# THE D'EVIL DIARIES

# HELL'S BELLES

ORCHARD BOOKS

First published in Great Britain in 2016 by The Watts Publishing Group

1 3 5 7 9 10 8 6 4 2

Text © Natasha Ellis 2016
Illustrations by Dave Shephard
© Orchard Books 2016

A CIP catalogue record for this book is available from the British Library.

ISBN 978 1 40833 578 9

Printed in Great Britain

MIX
Paper from
responsible sources
FSC® C104740

The paper and board used in this book are made from wood from responsible sources

Orchard Books
An imprint of Hachette Children's Group
Part of The Watts Publishing Group Limited
Carmelite House, 50 Victoria Embankment, London EC4Y 0DZ

An Hachette UK Company
www.hachette.co.uk
www.hachettechildrens.co.uk

# THE D'EVIL DIARIES

# HELL'S BELLES

## TATUM FLYNN

ORCHARD

# Contents

'The mind is its own place, and in it self
Can make a Heav'n of Hell, a Hell of Heav'n.'

John Milton, *Paradise Lost*

*To: Persephone*
*Villa Anoixi*
*Parga*
*Greece*

*Dear Mum,*

*Hope you're having a lovely holiday. Dad told me he came to visit you, I bet you were surprised! I was, anyway.* ~~*Since I was busy nearly getting killed about a hundred different ways at the time*~~*. About him coming to visit you, that is. Not anything else. Everything's been totally fine here. Yup. Nothing out of the ordinary at all.*

*I do have a new friend, though.* ~~*I ran away and*~~ *We... went on a school trip to Outer Hell and I bumped into this girl.* ~~*While I was busy saving Hell from a massive demon army and my rubbish older brother.*~~ *A Bonehead. I know that sounds weird, but I bet you'd like her, she's pretty kickass.* ~~*Luckily for me, or I'd be horse food.*~~ *Her name is Tommy. She's only eleven so she wasn't supposed to be in Hell. Since mistakes make Dad go all red-eyed and growly,*

7

*he invited her to stay in Darkangel Palace. In fact, me and Dad are throwing a birthday party for her tonight.*

*So, as you can see, Dad's changed quite a lot. Maybe you'll come home more often now that he's being nicer. Though they need you on Earth to make spring happen and stuff, I guess.*

*Anyway, see you soon. Loiter says hi. I miss you.*

*Jinx X*

# 1

# Happy Unbirthday to Me

TOMMY

IT'S A BIT weird having a birthday party when you're dead.

Especially when that party takes place in a pointy black palace in Hell, the guests are all demons, and most of all because, strictly speaking, you're not getting any older. Ever. Because dead.

But I wasn't complaining. I'd been in Hell a while now – ever since a teensy accident with my uncle and a circus lion – and although it probably sounds strange, I liked it here. OK, there was some scary stuff – homicidal witches, bottomless abysses, people's obnoxious older brothers trying to take over the world, that kind of thing.

Still, it wasn't so bad. And my new best friend Jinx was pretty great, even if he was the literal spawn of Satan.

I fiddled with a ribbon on my dress and looked down the wide marble staircase that led to the ballroom, which was crammed with a whirling kaleidoscope of faces. The Devil definitely knew how to throw a party. Demons of every

9

colour and kind – grey, blue, red; cat-faced, dragon-bodied, cloven-hooved – drank and danced and ate tiny cakes in the shape of throwing stars and daggers. On a stage in the middle of the room, a band fronted by a rhino-headed demon with a rumbling voice like a rock fall belted out song after song. Three vast red chandeliers swayed above the crowd, crystal tinkling like drops of frozen blood, and a writhing snake dropped from one of them onto – wait, what? Why were there snakes? Nobody told me there'd be snakes.

*Booksnakes.* That's what they'd be – just harmless book-eating snakes. Although we weren't in the library, so that was odd. It must have got lost. Or maybe it was friends with the weird octopussy creatures slithering across the tables around the dance floor, holding up glowing light bulbs in each tentacle like living candelabras.

Beyond the arched windows, the red marble towers of my new home city of Pandemonium gleamed gently in the fading evening light. I stuck my chin out and walked slowly down the staircase, trying to act posh and grown-up and like I belonged, even if I *was* the only human guest. Five more steps. Two. Phew, made it. I spun round, looking for Jinx. Then I tripped over a chair leg and went flying.

A balding waiter grabbed my elbow just before I hit the ground.

'Thanks,' I said.

He bowed nervously. Being served by damned humans – I guessed he was a glutton, since he was serving food he'd never get to eat – was really weird. I mean, I was a damned human too, even if I was here by mistake.

The balding waiter offered me a platter of tiny wriggling things on skewers.

'Ew.' Had I said that out loud? I'd said that out loud. I scrambled for something else to say. 'So, um…how did you die?'

His eyes grew wide.

OK, maybe that wasn't the best icebreaker.

'I was killed by lychees,' he mumbled, looking at his feet.

'Leeches?'

'No, lychees. Choked to death in a Chinese restaurant.'

I clamped my lips shut to keep from laughing. 'Oh. Right.'

'If that'll be all, miss…' He bowed again and sped off into the crowd.

So much for trying to act grown-up. I sat down. Sitting was safer.

Unless you sit on a snake.

'Aargh!' I jumped up to see a disgruntled-looking viper slither hurriedly away. What was it with the snakes?

Just then, Jinx squeezed through the crowd, looking as uncomfortable as any twelve-year-old boy who'd been forced to wear a tuxedo would look. I breathed a sigh of relief.

'Who invited snakes to my party?' I said, pointing furiously in the direction of the viper who'd presumably gone off to dance.

'Snakes? What snakes?'

'That's what I keep saying!' I huffed. 'Never mind.' I sat back down, more carefully this time.

Jinx flopped into a chair next to me. 'So! What do you think?' He gestured vaguely at the milling crowd.

Two red-skinned demons in ball gowns and a dog-headed demon in a tweed suit were looking at me with undisguised contempt. I bit my lip.

'I think posh parties in palaces might be even scarier than mad witches and dangerous libraries and carnivorous carousel horses.'

'Come on, nothing's scarier than carnivorous carousel horses.'

'True. Remind me how on Earth we ended up friends when you dragged me through all that?'

'Because I'm an awesome superhero who saved Hell?'

I narrowed my eyes.

'Er, an awesome superhero who saved Hell but couldn't have possibly done it without your help?'

'That's more like it.'

When I'd first met Jinx, I was living in a run-down shack in a grim, blizzardy place called The Fields of the Damned, a kind of shanty town scattered outside the towering walls of the city. After some hair-raising adventures I'm pretty sure will give me nightmares forever, I ended up living in his house. Or rather, palace. Like, a real, turrety, dungeons-and-all castle, perched on a rocky outcrop overlooking the demonic city of Pandemonium like an evil bat. It's so cool. Not that I'd tell him that. Boy's got a big enough head since all that hero-who-saved-Hell stuff happened.

'Anyway, you're like one of the family now,' he said. 'You'll get used to all this stuff.'

'Except I'm a dead human and everyone else is live demons and traditionally demons hate humans,' I pointed out.

He grinned. 'Well, yes, apart from that.'

'Seriously, this is brilliant. Thanks for talking your dad into it.' I smoothed out my shiny dress. 'And thanks for the new clothes. You have no idea how glad I am to get out of that smelly duffel coat.'

'It *was* a bit smelly.'

'I did die in it.'

'Excuses, excuses.' I fake scowled and he laughed. 'I'm glad you like the party. I was a bit nervous about living up to a circus.'

On Earth, back when I was alive, I'd worked in a travelling circus, under the iron fist of my Uncle Boozy, the ringleader-cum-slave-driver. Because my parents had abandoned me, I wasn't even sure when my birthday was. When I'd mentioned my sad lack of birthday shenanigans in passing to Jinx, he'd insisted on throwing me my first ever party. Stuff like that is why he's my best friend, even if he does have red skin and pointy horns and little black wings that fold out like an umbrella.

'Plus Dad didn't need much persuading,' Jinx said. 'He loves parties. Look.'

I followed his pointing finger to the stage. Lucifer had taken the microphone from the rhino and was in the middle of a fiery rendition of 'Bad Moon Rising'.

I snorted. 'Your dad is awesome.'

'He's always smiley this time of year, 'cos Mum's home soon. Oh, I nearly forgot. Happy Birthday!' He rummaged in a pocket for a moment and pulled out a small stone box – a small stone box with holes in it, and an arrow saying THIS WAY UP.

'Are those…breathing holes?' I said.

'Could be.'

I waved my hands in front of me. 'Oh no. If this is your idea of a joke, giving me some tentacled hellbeast as a present…'

His face fell.

I stared at him. 'It really is a tentacled hellbeast?'

'Look, just open it. It won't hurt you, promise. And if you don't like it I'll take it back to the shop and we can get something else, OK?'

I took the box and just held it for a moment. It was the first birthday present I'd ever been given. And it might try to kill me. Great.

I opened it reluctantly.

In the box, nestled on a small mound of red seaweed, sat a tiny blue creature with big, cute eyes. Big, cute eyes and… tentacles. Tentacles that were throwing off sparks. 'Oh, it's brilliant, thank you! It's so sweet, it's…'

Jinx's shoulders shook with laughter. 'You don't know what it is, do you?'

'I, in fact, do not know what it is, no,' I said. But it didn't look like it could eat me, so that was a bonus.

He pointed at a candelabra as it slithered down the table. 'It's a shocktopus! A baby one. It isn't big enough to power light bulbs yet. But if you tickle it under its chin, it'll glow. It's like a pocket torch.'

I took a breath and picked it up. 'Ow!'

'Oh yeah, it can shock you, be careful. Don't give me that death stare. It won't do it once it gets to know you. It's just a bit scared.'

I held the tiny creature in the palm of my hand and looked into its eyes. It stopped trying to electrocute me. There was even something that might have been a smile. 'I

shall name you Sparky. Thanks, Jinx.'

'Apart from being electricky, shocktopuses are really smart, you know.'

'Yeah?'

'Yeah. They can tell if someone nearby is lying. They send out a little spark or shock.'

Sparky had started to climb up my arm. 'Whoa. That is cool. I take back everything I said about tentacled hellbeasts.'

Jinx grinned. 'Thought you might like it.' He stood up, did a little mock bow in my direction and stuck his arm out. 'And now, m'lady, I do believe it's time to open the rest of your presents.'

I rolled my eyes but tucked my arm into his.

As we made our way across the room to a pile of presents beside the cascading staircase, I side-eyed Lucifer, now roaring out 'Highway to Hell'.

'Your dad's not going to make a speech, is he?'

'Oh, he never misses an opportunity to do that.'

I winced. I really didn't want to attract any more attention than I already had. Lucifer and Jinx had tried to make me feel at home, but I knew there were plenty of demons who were horrified that a Bonehead – what demons called damned humans – was living side-by-side with their Dark Lord. Plus there was the fact that kids never got sent here normally, so

17

that made everyone even more suspicious of me.

'Couldn't you persuade him not—'

A clash of cymbals echoed through the ballroom and the music and chatter came to an abrupt halt.

Every horned head in the glittering ballroom turned to their king.

My mouth went dry. 'Oh, *badgers.*'

Jinx snorted. 'Badgers?'

'It's a swearword on Earth.'

'I can never tell when you're taking the mickey.'

'Would I do that? I'll have you know badgers are dangerous carnivorous beasts.' Actually, when I'd worked in the circus some badgers had got into camp and eaten all our food one night. It had become a private joke, but I didn't feel like explaining it to Jinx just then. I was too busy quaking at the thought of Lucifer's speech.

'I just hope he doesn't tell any dad jokes,' Jinx muttered.

'They say pride comes before a fall, so I'd better watch my step,' began Lucifer, grinning and backing away from the edge of the stage.

Jinx groaned.

Lucifer tugged at the collar of his slick navy suit, looking as uncomfortable as Jinx for a second, despite being eight foot tall and built like a dragon on steroids. He cleared his throat. 'Humans aren't so bad, really,' he said.

You could have heard a pin drop. Or a spikemoth sneeze. The whole room went deathly quiet. Was he really being nice about demons' most hated enemy?

'After all,' he continued smoothly, 'if we didn't have Boneheads to torment here in Hell, and humans to corrupt over on Earth, life would be terribly dull, wouldn't it?'

The crowd broke into relieved laughter.

'All the same, every once in a millennium, a human comes along who is fit to rank amongst the finest demons. And today we are here to celebrate the birthday of one such person, Tomasina Covelli.'

Demons swivelled to stare at me. My cheeks were now glowing so hard I could've moonlighted as a shocktopus. I prayed Lucifer wouldn't ask me up on stage.

'Tommy not only played a crucial part in keeping the realm safe from our recent traitors, she also chose to stay here in Hell instead of the Other Place.'

A shudder passed through the throng at the mention of Heaven.

Lucifer held up a large red hand to silence them. 'And most importantly, she fed her nasty uncle to a circus lion. Which I think you'll agree shows remarkable talent for a girl who was only eleven at the time.'

There were scattered chuckles.

'So before I embarrass the girl any more, I'd like you to raise your glasses and drink a toast to Tommy's twelfth birthday, and,' – he unfurled his mighty wings suddenly, causing three green-skinned demons near the stage to take a step back – 'to remind you that anyone who does not welcome her here will be seen as a traitor. And I don't need to remind you what happens to traitors.'

The dog-headed demon in the tweed suit gulped.

Then everyone was toasting me and wishing me happy birthday and the band launched into a new song and it was over. Lucifer jumped down from the stage and strode over to us.

'Thank you, Your Badness,' I said.

Up close, the King of Hell towered over me like a friendly Godzilla. Although he'd probably laid waste to cities before too, so it didn't do to get too starry-eyed.

'You're most welcome. Time for presents?'

A long, razor-sharp set of claws gripped me by the shoulder. I spun round and came face to face with two big brown eyes. 'Loiter! You came.'

Loiter was Jinx's other best friend. He was an actual sloth, due to being the Patron Demon of Sloth, or Laziness, and one of the nicest demons in Hell, since he usually couldn't be bothered to be evil. He smiled lazily at us. 'But of course. Happy Birthday, Tommy, my dear.'

The four of us made our way across the ballroom, Lucifer leading the way, demons in their finery parting like scuttling ants before him.

I stroked Sparky, who was now sitting on my shoulder. He wasn't slimy, like an earthly octopus, but smooth, almost silky to the touch. 'Is this the best day ever, or what?' I said, beaming. A tiny shock ran through my collar bone. 'Hey! What was that about?' Maybe he was still a bit nervous.

I turned back to the others. Lucifer plucked a huge box from the small mountain of presents and said, 'Go on, open it, open it!' with a grin on his face like a little kid.

Loiter and I sat down on the bottom step and Jinx scooted along next to us as I ripped off the shiny crimson paper. Beneath was a carved wooden chest, banded with iron like something out of a pirate story. Although, knowing Lucifer, he'd actually got it from real pirates. I swung it open and gasped.

Inside sat row upon row of shiny throwing stars and tiny daggers, neatly arranged in black silk. When I'd worked in the circus, I'd been a knife thrower, and my skills had come in pretty handy surviving Hell.

'Wow. That's quite an arsenal,' said Jinx.

I plucked out a star-shaped hira-shuriken and turned it in my hand. It was light as a feather and sharp as death. 'Oh, this is amazing! Thank you so much!' I jumped up and to my own surprise, gave Lucifer a big hug. If his face hadn't already been red, I would've sworn he blushed.

He waved me away. 'Oh, nothing, you know, just a tiny—'

All of a sudden, every light flickered and went out, and the ballroom was plunged into pitch blackness. The band ground to a screechy halt and murmurs filled the air.

*Uh oh.*

On the bright side, I had the Devil himself standing right next to me, so what was there really to be afraid of?

'What's going on?' I whispered to Jinx. Or possibly the banister, since I couldn't actually see him.

At the top of the stairs, a blue light began to glow. The blue glow turned into blue flames – hellfire – and in the midst of the flames appeared a person... Or rather a demon... Or a queen. I didn't know what to think.

She was the most beautiful woman I'd ever seen. Skin as pale as moonlight, and somehow as cold, long black hair that floated *up* as though she were underwater, and a glittering black dress covered with thousands of tiny black pearls. Tiny, black pearls that seemed to be swarming all over her. I gulped. The queen-woman-thing paused for

a moment, looking out over the darkened ballroom, and smiled – but it was the cut-throat smile of someone who stuck pins in live butterflies. And we were the butterflies.

Then with a wave of her hand, all the lights flamed back to life and the party slowly started up once more. Now I saw the wings sprouting from her back – not one set like Jinx and most demons, but two, shimmering like deep green snakeskin. The terrifying swarmy demon glided down the steps towards us. I decided total cowardice was the better

23

part of valour and hid behind Lucifer.

'Ah, Lilith, you always did like to make an entrance,' said the King of Hell, sounding amused.

Jinx, however, looked like he'd swallowed a razorbug.

The woman held out her hand and Lucifer bent to kiss it. 'Well, it would be unkind of me not to brighten everyone's evening a little with my presence, wouldn't it?' she said. She had a hissing way of speaking that sent shivers down my spine.

'And it has been so very long since you last graced us with that presence,' said Loiter, ambling forward. 'To what do we owe the honour?'

'Ah, Loiter, how good to see you,' she said. 'Well, I do like to pop by and see my children from time to time, you know.' She shrugged casually.

'Every few centuries,' said Lucifer, his voice still dripping with amusement.

'Quite, mustn't coddle them.' Her eyes alighted on me. 'And who might this be? The birthday girl, I presume?'

I wondered how she knew.

Lucifer pushed me forward. 'Ah, yes, this is Tommy, a rather special case.'

'I bet you are.' Lilith bent down from her great height – she was almost as tall as Lucifer, although several inches

24

of that was a pair of pointed black stilettos that looked like they doubled as weapons – and smiled at me like a lion might smile at an antelope with a broken leg. 'Happy birthday, Tommy, delighted to meet you.'

Close up, I now saw not only that the swarming black pearls were tiny wandering beetles, but that Lilith had the yellow, black-slitted eyes of a serpent. If Lucifer hadn't been standing right next to me I might've peed my pants. Yet despite everything, there was something magnetic about her. My tongue stuck to the roof of my mouth but I managed to mumble something polite.

Then she tucked her arm into Lucifer's, whispered something in his ear, and whisked him off into the crowd, leaving me, Jinx and Loiter gaping after her.

'Who *was* that?' I said.

'*That*,' replied Jinx, frowning so hard I thought his forehead might crack, 'was Dad's first wife, Lilith. You might know her better as the serpent from the Garden of Eden.'

'Oh,' I said. 'Ohhh.'

Well, at least that explained the snakes.

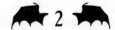

## 2

# A Fiend in Need

TOMMY

## THE DEAD GIRL'S GUIDE TO HELL

· You don't need to eat or drink. Because dead.

· Which doesn't mean you *can't*, if a particularly tasty grimberry cupcake happens to fall into your lap.

· You look the same as you did when you were alive. Not like a ghost, or a skeleton, or a zombie. Which is nice.

· You can't fly or walk through walls. Disappointing.

· You're dead, so you can't die again. But if you get an arm bitten off by a hellbeast, it won't magically grow back. Even more disappointing.

· You can get sucked into Hell by accident if your no-good uncle sells his soul to the Devil and you happen to be nearby when he pops his clogs.

OK, THAT LAST one probably only applied to me. I crossed it out and chewed the end of my pen thoughtfully. Writing is harder than it looks. But if any other human ever ended up in Hell by accident like I'd done, maybe my guide could help them. Not that it was likely. At all. The truth was...what was the truth?

The truth was I was *acclimatising*, which was a long word Loiter had taught me meaning 'to get used to something really weird'. Humans weren't supposed to live happily ever after in Hell. That wasn't what it was here for. So I was having to learn how to do something no one else had ever done – and judging by some of the sly looks and whispered comments at the party, something a lot of demons were hoping I'd never manage to do.

But writing stuff down helped me figure it out. Like laying out all the jigsaw pieces before you start. If I could just find the corners, I'd be fine.

Outside my leaded bedroom window, the fiery moat crackled softly far below, the odd wisp of ash floating past in the green morning light. On my desk, Sparky trailed across a piece of paper, leaving burn marks in his wake. I suddenly remembered Hellish ink was made from kraken wee and took the pen out of my mouth. Well, there was something else to put in the guide.

'⚰♥☗☗☜ ☾☞♯♯⚖,' said a voice that sounded like sandpaper rubbing on stone. '☒♥☗☗☜☏☜☷☗☗ ♯☞←☀☏☀Υ ☷☞← ☗ ☗☏☏☜☜☗☗♥ ☜♥☒☜☏ ☗☀☜ ☜♥☗☜←☗☗☜☏☀.'

I stuck my head out the window and smiled. 'Hello, Grrr.' Grrr was a gargoyle with the head of a lion and wings of an eagle. 'It *is* a beautiful morning.'

'♯☞←☀☏☀Υ,' said another voice.

I turned to the skull-faced, bat-winged gargoyle hopping along the wall. 'Morning, Argg.' Jinx had been teaching me Gargoylish. I still only knew a few words, but Grrr and Argg had been helping me. Which isn't to say I hadn't screamed like a little boy the first time they'd tried to talk to me. I blushed thinking about it.

- Gargoyles are probably the friendliest creatures in Hell. They like to chat. A lot.

- They can hop around, but have to stay on their own building.

- The palace gargoyles look down on all the other gargoyles. In fact, they can be hilariously snooty for stone creatures with faces like squished rats.

I chewed absent-mindedly on a split end as Grrr and Argg started to discuss the finer points of philosophy. Or possibly

the finer points of football. I always did get those two words muddled up.

There was a knock at the door. I stuffed the pages in a desk drawer and jumped up. I didn't want Jinx to know I felt out of place. He'd feel bad, and I didn't want that, especially after the cool party he'd thrown me the night before.

But it wasn't Jinx at the door.

A grey messenger demon handed me an envelope,

nodded politely, then flew off before I could say a word. Huh. *Miss Tomasina Covelli* was written on the front in curling red ink. Or possibly blood. I ripped it open and stared. Then I dashed straight down the corridor to Jinx's room, threw open the door...and ran right into him, knocking him to the floor.

'Ow!' He rubbed his head, then looked up and smirked. 'Nice cupcake pyjama trousers.'

'Shut up.' I grabbed his hand and pulled him to his feet. 'Have you seen this?' I waved the stiff piece of paper under his nose.

'I was just coming to see you about it,' he said. 'Before you decided to use me for tenpin bowling practice.'

---

# INVITATION

## TO ALL CHILDREN OF THE DEMONOCRACY
## SECOND FORM TO FIFTH FORM

You are cordially invited to attend a talk by
### *Her Majestic Fiendishness, Lilith*

LOCATION: *Salome Hall, third floor, Darkangel Palace*
TIME: *Noon today*
OF PARTICULAR INTEREST TO: *The bravest, most evil demons in the realm. And anyone interested in a career in corruption.*

Refreshments will be provided.　　　　　　　　　RSVP not necessary.

---

'Guess we're going to find out what Snake Lady is doing here.'

'Loiter told me this is the first time she's visited Hell in over four hundred years. Why come back now? She's up to something, I can feel it in my horns.'

I grinned.

He looked suspiciously at me. 'Why are you smiling?'

'No reason. I'm going to get dressed. See you in a bit.'

The truth was I was smiling because at that moment I couldn't have cared less what Lucifer's first wife was doing in Hell. I'd been invited to something all the other demon children had been invited to – me, a human, a *Bonehead*. My name was written right on the envelope, so there was no mistake. Maybe fitting in in Hell wasn't going to be so hard after all.

An hour later, the two of us trekked through the palace to Salome Hall. On Earth I'd lived in a cramped, grubby trailer, so Darkangel Palace was taking some getting used to. My knowledge of palaces came strictly from Disney films, but there weren't any dancing teapots or singing bluebirds here. Every inch of wall was covered in beautiful murals, or carved wood or marble, or curly gold bits, but the art was less 'blue skies and cherubs' and more 'monsters bloodily ripping someone's head off'. All the ceilings were so far above my head you could've had a bouncy castle in every room. I made a mental note to put in a request for at least one.

'You look tired,' I said to Jinx as we made our way down yet another stone staircase.

He made a face. 'Couldn't sleep. Kept dreaming about snakes.'

'Oh. So tell me more about your mysterious snakey stepmother. Or whatever you call someone's first wife. Is Lilith the mother of your brothers and sisters? All 665 of them?'

'Nah, not all of them. Dad's had other girlfriends. But my mum and Lilith were the only ones he married.'

'And you're Persephone's only son, right?'

'Yep. So I'm the only half-demon in the family. At least, I think so.'

'So why do you think Lilith's turned up now?'

Jinx headed down a hallway lined with gigantic gold mirrors, and I followed. 'It's been centuries. So, I've never met her before, although I recognised her from paintings. No one seems to know why she's here. It's fishy, if you ask me.'

'It's probably nothing. Not everyone is plotting to take over Hell, you know.'

He scowled. 'Dantalion was.'

Dantalion was Jinx's older brother who'd tried to take over from Lucifer. It hadn't turned out well for him.

There was a squeak and a small vampire bat flapped down the corridor after us and landed on Jinx's shoulder.

'Hello, Bruce,' I said, reaching up to stroke him. 'So, Jinx, what about your mum? I can't imagine she'd be too happy to know Lilith's swanning round the castle.'

Jinx shrugged. 'Probably not. But she's home on Fienday. Not long.'

'I know your mum's, like, some kind of goddess of spring on Earth—'

'She makes spring happen,' said Jinx proudly. 'Earth wouldn't survive without her.'

'But what does she do when she's down here? Just lounge around pining for sunshine?'

He jerked his chin back, offended. 'Course not. She's the Queen of the Dead! She weighs all the souls and decides who goes where. She's basically in charge when she's here. Only person Dad ever takes orders from, not that he'd admit it. In olden days, people weren't even allowed to say her name. She's the Scourge of the Underworld, She Who

Must Not Be Named, the Terror of the Boneheads!' By this point he was waving his hands around, all hot under the collar.

'Whoa, easy, tiger. I'm sure she's badass.'

'She is. You just wait and see how things change when she gets back.'

Jinx headed on down a long black corridor lined with horned suits of armour, Bruce hovering above, but suddenly I couldn't move. A cold, swirling pit opened up in my belly at the thought of things changing. *The Terror of the Boneheads*. How was she going to react to finding a Bonehead living under her roof? What if she kicked me out?

'When did you say your mum's back?' I called to him.

'Fienday.'

Fienday. It was Sinday today – I had almost got used to the Hellish days of the week now, although Worseday still made me giggle – so that meant I only had five days until Persephone returned. Five days to...what? To show I could demon with the best of them. To fit in. It was suddenly way more urgent.

Jinx stopped. 'You all right?'

What was I supposed to say? *You've just told me your mum is the Queen of the Dead and hates Boneheads, so not really? I've already been abandoned by one mum so I don't have a lot of faith in them? You're my best friend and I don't want to lose you?* But Jinx and Lucifer were so excited about Persephone coming back, I didn't want to rain on their parade. And maybe I was worrying about nothing. Maybe. I changed the subject. 'So if Lilith doesn't live in Hell, what does she do?'

'She lives on Earth. She's in charge of all the fiends.'

I caught up to Jinx and we carried on walking. 'The fiends are the ones who corrupt humans, right?' There were a bunch of different kinds of demons and I had a hard time keeping track of them all.

'Yep. You'll see in a minute.'

We rounded a corner and I followed Jinx into what I presumed was Salome Hall. By the time we got there, it was teeming with hundreds of demon kids, mostly red-skinned like Jinx, although none with his smiley blue eyes. I could hardly hear a thing above the roar of chatter and anticipation, and the screech of chairs on floorboards. We slipped into seats near the back just as four of the weirdest-looking creatures I'd ever seen slunk onto the stage at the front.

'Ugh. Glad we're back here so we can't smell them,' said Jinx.

The creatures were skinny as pipe-cleaners, with pale skin so thin you could see the blue blood pumping through their veins, like a slice of blue cheese. Unlike every other demon I'd seen, they didn't wear clothes. Well, Loiter didn't either, but I suspected that was just because he was too lazy to ever get dressed. I'd seen a lot of creepy things in Hell, but the things up on stage were definitely up there with the creepiest.

'Are those fiends?' I whispered. 'And what do you mean, smell them?'

Jinx nodded. 'They always smell of brimstone, kind of a rotten-egg stink. It's really gross.'

'Ew.'

'Silence for Her Majestic Fiendishness, Lilith!' screeched the tallest fiend. He had a single greasy coil of black hair that fell across his head like a dead crow, and a dripping nose he kept wiping. The chatter in the room ebbed to a low murmur.

Lilith glided onstage in a dark green leather jacket and jeans, black ringlets coiling up into the air, her wings glistening in the light.

'I detest speeches,' she hissed. The words seemed to snake round the walls of the hall until they were whispering right in my ear. I shivered.

'So I shall get straight to the point. I need a new assistant in the Department of Corruption and Temptation. Someone clever and resourceful who can oversee my fiends and help me expand the realm's evil activities. Someone like *you*.'

Again the words felt like they were being whispered right into my ear. I glanced at Jinx but his eyes were fixed on Lilith. Could he hear them too? Or was I imagining things?

'To help me choose, there will be a contest, open to demons aged twelve to fifteen. You are no longer children, but you are young enough not to have chosen your area of speciality yet, unlike the sixth formers.'

A contest? The ears of every demon in the room pricked up. Demons were nothing if not competitive. Any excuse for a fight.

'The competition will be divided into three parts: Physical Prowess, Intelligence, and Resourcefulness. If you wish to rise to the position of my deputy one day, you will need to prove your ability in all three arenas. The contest will take place at various locations around Pandemonium, and will begin on Moanday, in other words tomorrow.'

She clapped her hands loudly. 'Any questions?'

A lanky, red-skinned demon in the front row raised his hand. 'Will the, um, assistant position be based on Earth?'

'Yes. You will live in my fortress in the Himalayas.'
She smiled. 'But there will be plenty of travel, including
returning occasionally to Hell. Anything else?'

Silence.

'Does no one wish to know if the contest will be
dangerous?' she drawled, eyeing the students before her.

Nobody dared to reply.

'Well, it will be. A timid deputy is of no use to me. So
if you are brave enough, join me and my staff at the Evil
Eyrie, tomorrow at two o'clock. I look forward to culling
the sheep from the wolves.' She swooped offstage.

The room erupted into chatter once more and Jinx and
I jumped up to beat the queue out.

'See, told you she didn't have some dastardly plan,' I
said as we made our way down the hallway. 'It's just a job
interview, Hell-style.'

Jinx frowned. 'Hmm, maybe. I still don't trust her.'

I didn't want to admit it to Jinx, but I thought she was
the coolest thing I'd ever seen. And she'd invited me to take
part in her contest.

Jinx stopped and looked at me. 'Why are you looking all
think-y? Do you have a plan for—'

*The Terror of the Boneheads,* I thought. Persephone
would be here in five days. This could be my chance to

prove I belonged. 'I'm going to enter the contest.' The words were out before I could stop myself. 'And you're coming with me.'

PERCIVAL

*Percival wiped his nose on his sleeve as he left Salome
Hall, and slunk sulkily back to his room on the ground
floor of the East Wing. He sank onto the bed but a
mattress spring stuck into his skinny behind and he
got up again, grumbling. Why were beds in strange
places never as comfortable as your own? Instead
he wandered over to the window, but he didn't even
have a nice view of Pandemonium – just a muddy*

*courtyard backing onto some dragon stables.*

*He sighed. He hadn't wanted to come to Hell. He especially hadn't wanted to come to Hell just so he could watch some spoilt brat take the deputy job that by rights should've been his.*

*Why couldn't Lilith see what an excellent deputy he'd make? He'd been the Demon Resources Manager for four centuries now. He knew all the ins and outs of staff chastisement and temptation quotas and corruption enhancement. True, he'd been stuck behind a desk since 1541, but when he'd been out on the streets he'd had one of the highest success ratings of any fiend. He was the one who'd persuaded William the Conqueror to invade England, damn it.*

*He sniffed again. To add insult to injury, he had a cold, despite the fact the palace was far warmer than Lilith's fortress in the Himalayas. He hoped he wasn't coming down with something worse. Then, out of the corner of his eye, he spotted something – or rather someone.*

*A slim, green-skinned demon with tall curving horns like an antelope stood by the stable door, stroking one of the dragons. A rather lovely green-skinned demon. Percival suddenly wasn't so sorry to be in Hell after all.*

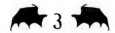

# 3

# Art Attack

JINX

I STARED AT Tommy. 'You want to do *what*?'

Dozens of pointy-tailed kids pushed us this way and that down the hall. Tommy grabbed my arm and pulled me into a side room. Which turned out to be a broom cupboard. A sponge fell on my head.

Tommy snorted and dragged me back out and into the next room, which was a small library, shut the door and leant against it. 'I want to take part in the contest. Come on, I bet it'll be fun.'

I tried to keep the hurt off my face. 'But...but you've just settled in here. And you want to leave already? You want to go and live in the Himalayas?'

'Oh no. Of course not! I love it here. I just think it'll be a laugh, that's all.'

I narrowed my eyes. 'There's something you're not telling me.'

She blew her fringe out of her eyes and perched on the

edge of an armchair. 'There isn't,' she said. 'Honest. It's nice to be asked, that's all. Me, a *Bonehead*. I just want to fit in here, Jinx, surely you can understand that?'

I thought about all the times I'd been bullied for accidentally being Good. All the times I'd felt like an outcast. 'Of course I can.' I shrugged. 'But it might be dangerous.'

She grinned. 'That's why I need you! You're my partner-in-crime. We saved Hell together, remember?'

'And nearly got killed a hundred times trying to do it,' I grumbled.

'And whose fault was that?'

She had me there. I did kind of owe her. Kind of a lot.

'And,' she said, 'if you're worried Lilith is up to something, this way we can keep an eye on her.'

'I'd been hoping for more of a stealth assignment,' I muttered. Not a death-defying one. 'Let me think about it.'

She leapt to her feet. 'I know! We can ask your dad about it. I mean, he wouldn't let it happen if it was really dangerous, would he?'

'Um. Tommy, I know my dad rules, but I think you're forgetting that he is literally the Devil.'

'Look, let's just see what he says. He'll know whether this contest is rated XXX or just "scenes of mild peril".'

I didn't like the way this was going. But I could still

say no. In fact, whatever Dad said, I was going to say no anyway. I liked being alive. But I owed it to Tommy to at least pretend to think about it. 'OK.'

We bundled back out into the hallway and up three flights of stairs to Dad's study. Tommy rapped the door knocker. There was no reply.

I backed away. 'Oh, he's out! What a shame. Let's come back another ti—'

'Enter!' boomed a voice.

Dammit.

Tommy pushed open the door and I followed reluctantly.

'Hi, Dad,' I said with a sigh. Then I did a double take.

The King of Hell was sitting on the floor surrounded by piles of wrapping paper, ribbons, and Damnazon boxes. A little piece of Sellotape was stuck to one curving horn.

'Hello, kids! What's up?'

I took a step forward. 'We wanted to ask you about...um, that is... Dad, what are you doing?'

'What does it look like? Wrapping presents.'

'Christmas presents? It's only October,' said Tommy.

'Well, Damnazon can be a bit slow with deliveries,' he said. 'I like to be organised.'

'But...*Christmas* presents?' I repeated, confused. For obvious reasons, we didn't celebrate Christmas in Hell.

Dad stood up and shook a piece of ribbon free from one wing. 'Not exactly.' He shoved a gift tag under our noses. It read *Happy Saturnalia! From Satan xxx* 'I get a lot of letters every year, you see. From kids who aren't good at spelling.'

Tommy burst out laughing. 'You mean they write to Satan instead of Santa?'

'Yes, exactly. And for years I ignored them. But then I thought maybe I could do something useful with them. So now they all get a special gift from me.'

Tommy peered at the Damnazon boxes. 'Stink bombs, itching powder, *Hacking For Dummies*,' she read. 'Is that...is that a flamethrower?'

Dad studied his fingernails. 'Maybe.'

I snorted. 'Dad, you're a genius. Anyway, I wanted to ask you about this contest of Lilith's—'

'Oh yes? Actually, I've got a surprise for you.' He opened the door. 'Come with me. We can talk about the contest on the way.'

A surprise? That was...surprising. Right. We jogged after him down the corridor.

'So, this contest...Lilith said it'd be dangerous, but it won't really, will it?' asked Tommy. 'After all, we're just kids.'

Dad cackled. 'Ooh, I forgot you don't know Lilith. Oh no, I'm pretty sure it'll be *exceedingly* dangerous. She's a wild one, that woman.'

I narrowed my eyes at Tommy, who sped into damage limitation mode.

'Yes, but...I mean no one's going to get *eaten* or anything, are they?'

Dad paused at the top of a stairwell. 'Let me tell you a story about my lovely first wife. Once upon a time, many millennia ago, a city in Egypt sacrificed a thousand snakes to their gods. I think they just had a bit of trouble with pest control, actually, but they decided to turn it into an offering. As you can imagine, Lilith wasn't too happy about the demise of her slithery friends.' He paused dramatically and raised his eyebrows at us. 'So she turned all the citizens into mice, transformed into a giant serpent, and ate them. It was quite amusing.'

Tommy's shoulders slumped and she gave up.

I mentally thanked Dad for getting me out of a sticky spot.

A few minutes later we found ourselves in the basement, in a wide blue hallway I'd never been in before – not that that was a surprise. The palace was so mammoth, there were still several places I hadn't explored. Iron doors studded both sides. I looked at the brass plaques as Dad strode by. Computer Virus Lab. Human Virus Lab. Poison Testing. Monster Development. A growl echoed out from behind the last door. I made a note to stay well away from that room.

Dad glanced over his shoulder. 'Don't go poking around down here, OK, you two? These doors are locked for a reason.'

Tommy, who was suddenly looking a bit pale, nodded. Finally Dad came to a halt in front of a set of double doors at the end. A hammering sound came from behind them.

The plaque said *'Ars Longa, Vita Brevis'*. I had no clue what that meant, but if this floor was Hellish Research and Development, I was beginning to lose my curiosity about Dad's surprise.

Dad threw open the doors and led us inside. Tommy gasped, then sneezed so hard she whacked herself in the eye with a plait. We were in a vast, vaulted stone hall. Dust floated on the dry air. The back half of the room was taken up by shelves built almost up to the ceiling – shelves piled high with statues and busts and art of every kind. The front of the room, however, was busy with life. A dozen demons and Boneheads were hammering metal, sploshing paint and carving wood.

A smiling, white-bearded human came up to us. 'Your Majesty, 'ow may I 'elp you today?' he said in a thick French accent.

'Hello, Monsieur Rodin.' Dad pushed me in front of him.

'Ah, of course, the son! Come with me!' He nodded to me and Tommy. 'Welcome to our workshop. Finest art in Pandemonium!'

'All the art in the palace is created here,' said Dad. 'And the pieces we don't have room to display are stored until I feel like a change in decoration.'

We walked past a yellow-skinned demon who was

putting the final touches to a painting of a grumpy man pushing a boulder up a hill. Behind the man, a woman in black robes stood clutching a whip.

'Is that your mum?' said Tommy, pointing at the painting, a quiver in her voice.

'Yeah, cool, huh?'

Tommy didn't reply.

Rodin led us to something covered in a sheet.

'Ready for that surprise, Jinx?' said Dad.

'Um, yes?'

Rodin pulled off the cover with a flourish like a bullfighter.

On a plinth stood a marble statue of a small demon brandishing a sword in each hand, a knife between his teeth and a fierce look of determination on his face... A small demon who looked remarkably like me.

'A promise is a promise,' said Dad.

I bounced up and down. 'Whoa, that is so cool! And a whole statue, not just a bust! Thanks, Dad. Best surprise ever.'

Tommy snorted. 'I don't remember the part where you were armed to the teeth.'

'Shut up,' I said, grinning.

'Glad you like it. I'd better get back to wrapping those

presents. See you kids later.' Dad patted me on the shoulder,
smiled at Tommy, and strode off out of the room.

I walked around the statue, ogling every inch of my new,
heroic self.

Monsieur Rodin hovered beside us, watching.

Tommy scuffed a toe across the floor. 'So, um, how did
you end up here, Mr Rodin?'

'Ah, it is the fault of art, you see,' he said wistfully.

'Art?'

'My one true love. I sold my soul for talent. Now I am

remembered as the greatest sculptor in all of France, but...'

'But you're here.'

He shrugged. 'Is not so bad, eh? I am still creating art. I am quite 'appy.'

Tommy beamed at him. Maybe she was pleased to find at least one other Bonehead enjoying their afterlife in Hell.

'You perhaps know my work?' he said to me.

'Oh yes,' I lied, 'I love your stuff, especially...'

'My gates of 'ell? They were very popular.'

'Yup, those. Brilliant.'

'I model the entrance to Lucifer's study after them.'

I thought of the snakes and goblins and gargoyles carved on the doors. 'Cool.'

'What's that?' asked Tommy, pointing at a brass machine like a cement mixer with a pointed rubber nozzle snaking away from it.

'Ah, my new toy! I call it the Art Rocket. Is filled with quick-setting plaster of Paris.' He picked up the nozzle and pointed it at me, and I took a step backwards. 'I use to make the rococo decorations for the ceilings.'

'You mean the gold curly bits?' said Tommy.

Rodin smiled. 'Yes. Much easier now.'

I went back to mooning over the statue of me in all my glory, but Tommy peered curiously around the room.

'Can we have a look around?' she said.

'But of course,' said Rodin, 'though please not to touch anything, eh?'

I left Heroic Me behind and followed Tommy further into the room. It was massive – the shelves went back so far I couldn't see where they ended. The right-hand wall was entirely covered with paintings. There were several of Lilith – no doubt banished to the storeroom by Mum – including a huge one of a city full of mice with a massive serpent looming over them. I thought of Dad's story and shivered. No way was I taking part in the contest now. If that was Tommy's idea of fun, that was up to her. I was going to stay well out of it. I trailed along, admiring various scenes of blood and gore, a statue of a dragon made of knives, and a table-sized model of the Labyrinth made out of matchsticks.

My stomach rumbled loudly. 'Come on,' I said, 'let's go get some lunch.'

Tommy grimaced. 'It better not be those eyeball things again.'

'You're dead, you don't need to eat anyway. Just leave them.'

She flushed. 'I was trying to be polite.'

'This is Hell. You don't have to worry about politeness.'

'Yeah, a *palace* in Hell,' she said. 'With about fifteen different forks to choose from. I don't know if that's a Hellish thing or just a posh thing, but I'm not used to it.'

'Dad eats like a starving wolf and Loiter eats with his paws. You have better manners than both of them.'

She nudged me in the ribs. 'Thanks.'

I turned back towards the front of the workshop and tripped over a bolt of green velvet trailing from a shelf. A small painting clattered to the floor. Oops. I picked it up and leant it against the wall.

Tommy and I stared at each other, open-mouthed.

In the painting was a young woman with blonde hair and brown eyes, holding a box. A young woman who looked exactly like Tommy.

## 4

# Kittens and Chickens

TOMMY

'WHY,' SAID A frowning Jinx, 'is there a picture of you in Hell?'

'Nope nope nope.' I glared at the woman in the painting. 'I'm in Hell because my stupid uncle sold his soul to your dad and I got caught in the crossfire. End of story. I do *not* need any new mysteries.' I rubbed the dust off the frame and peered at the inscription below. '*Pandora*. So who's Pandora and why does she have my face?'

Jinx's eyes went wide. 'You must be related.' He jabbed his finger at me. 'You must have demon blood!'

'Don't be daft,' I said. 'I am not a demon.'

'What's wrong with being a demon?'

'Apart from being responsible for untold pain and misery and the invention of homework, you mean?'

'Homework isn't all…yeah, OK, never mind.'

I pointed at my bum. 'Anyway, I can't be a demon. Distinct lack of pointy tail.'

'Hmm. True.'

We looked around for Rodin but he'd disappeared.

'We can ask Dad,' said Jinx, heading out of the workshop, 'he might know.'

I hurried after him and dragged him to a stop halfway down the corridor. 'Don't.'

'Don't? Why?'

I shrugged, but my heart was beating fast. 'I don't know, I just…What if this Pandora person was an enemy of his or something?'

'Then why would he have a painting of her?' asked Jinx, perfectly reasonably. Then he smirked. 'More likely she was an ex.'

I smacked him on the shoulder. 'Not. Helping.'

'Maybe she was an ex and you're descended from Dad! We could be related!' He snorted with laughter, then stopped when he saw my face. 'Hey, I'm sorry, I'm only kidding. I'm sure you're as human as the next dead circus girl.'

Of course, being descended from Lucifer would solve all my problems about not belonging in Hell. But it would also mean being descended from Lucifer. As much as I wanted to fit in, I thought that was maybe taking things a bit far.

A sudden burst of squeaky miaowing came from the

door next to us. The door marked Monster Development.

'What was that?' said Jinx.

There was a small glass square in the door. Curiosity got the better of me and I stood on tiptoes and peered through. I burst out laughing.

'What?' Jinx pulled me out of the way and looked through.

'Kittens! *Kittens.* I really want to know how your dad is planning to wreak havoc on humanity with baby cats,' I said, strange paintings forgotten for a moment.

'Dad works in mysterious ways. Maybe they're going to befriend humans and ruin their lives by being so cute people's heads explode.'

'Or peeing on everything they love. Or wanting to go in and out so many times a day their owners are driven mad.'

'I'm pretty sure cats already do that.'

'Truth.'

'Come on, let's go and get something to eat.'

After lunch we trudged back upstairs, rabbiting about the mystery of my weird lookalike. I followed Jinx into his room and a furry head emerged from the hammock hanging from the rafters.

'Woke me up,' grumbled Loiter.

'Ha ha,' said Jinx. This was a running joke since

Loiter was almost always asleep.

'Loiter! Just the person I wanted to see.' I smiled at him.

'You're really not going to let me sleep, are you?' he grumbled.

'Nope. Do you know anything about a woman called Pandora? From ancient times. There's a painting of her in the art storeroom.'

'Pandora as in Pandora's Box, you mean?'

'Yes! How did you know about the box?' asked Jinx, sitting in his desk chair and spinning round.

I perched on the window seat and tucked my knees under my chin.

Loiter yawned. 'Why the sudden interest?'

Jinx raised an eyebrow at me.

'It's sort of a secret,' I said. 'For now.'

'She means don't tell Dad,' said Jinx helpfully.

'Ooh, well now you have my full attention,' said Loiter.

'Pandora looked just like me,' I said. 'Well, an older me.'

He waggled a long claw at me. 'Yes! Of course! I knew I'd seen you somewhere before.'

'So you knew her?' I said, flushed with excitement.

'Oh, no. I'm afraid not. I've just seen pictures.'

'Oh.'

'But I can tell you what I know. Pandora was a

human, not a demon.'

I breathed a huge sigh of relief.

'I saw that,' said Jinx.

'Not just any human, either,' continued Loiter, 'a famous queen, a long, long time ago. The story goes that she discovered a box filled with all the evils that exist. Despite being warned, she was too curious and opened it. All the evils flew out – misery, pride, pestilence, war, you name it – and infected the Earth. So basically, she's to blame for all the ills of the world.'

'Why can't I have a cuddly great-great-grandma who baked cookies and kept kittens?' I pouted. 'So that's why there's a painting of her? She was really evil?'

'I did say "so the story goes". I know there's more to the tale, but there have been so many different versions through the ages that all anyone remembers any more is Pandora, curiosity, box. Some say she was the first human on Earth, but that's just a fairy tale. The first human was a lot more cave-womanish. I think she was called Graah.'

'Graah?'

'Took humans a while to do more than just grunt. Backward species.'

'Hey!'

Loiter shrugged. 'Sorry. True, though.'

Jinx frowned. 'Wait, I thought Adam and Eve were the first humans. Garden of Eden and all that.'

'Nah, they just had better PR. No one wants to read about a bunch of cave people grunting at each other. Adam and Eve were just the first humans who were bright enough for us demons to care about. Naturally Lilith swooped in and corrupted them straight away. Humans were better off stupid.'

'Huh.' You really did learn interesting stuff in Hell.

Loiter yawned. 'Anyway, as for Pandora, I don't think even Lucifer remembers what really happened.'

I had an idea. 'I bet we can find out more in Babel.'

Loiter nodded. 'The library? Yes, perhaps.'

My heart skipped. If I really were descended from some cool evil queen, maybe I wouldn't have to worry about not fitting in. Maybe Persephone and all the demons who saw me as a hated Bonehead would come around. This was the answer to all my prayers, even though I hadn't known it!

'Brilliant. Thanks, Loiter.'

'No problem, my dear. So I heard about this contest of Lilith's – you two taking part?'

Jinx looked at the floor.

'I am,' I said, 'even though *some* people are too chicken.'

'I never understood that phrase, you know,' said Loiter.

'Chickens can be quite vicious. Why, once in Albania in the twelfth century there was this giant rooster—'

'I'm sleuthing,' interrupted Jinx. 'That's why I'm not taking part. I think Lilith's up to something.'

'Such as?' asked Loiter.

'Such as trying to take over Hell.'

I rolled my eyes.

Loiter tapped his claws together. 'I do understand that all the business with Dantalion was a nasty shock to you, Jinx,' he said gently. 'But try to remember your suspicions about Astaroth.'

Astaroth was a creepy lizard-headed demon who Jinx had thought had an Evil Plan. Turned out he hadn't at all. He was just creepy-looking.

'I know, I know,' said Jinx. 'I can still investigate, though.'

'But of course. Just don't count your pterodactyls before they hatch.'

Jinx squirmed. 'You want a refill?' he asked, jumping up from the bed.

'What? Oh, yes please.'

Jinx opened the fridge, took out a big jug of something that looked like banana milk and smelled like suntan oil, and tipped it into the tall vase Loiter was using as a glass. The sloth sucked on the straw that snaked all the way down

from the ceiling and gave a satisfied belch. 'If you're not into health food, if you have half a brain…' he sang off-key.

I stuck my tongue out at Jinx. 'I don't need your help anyway.' More like he needed mine. He'd never have saved Hell by himself, not that I got a statue for my pains. I clenched my fists. I'd show him. I could do this on my own. And then everyone would see that humans were just as good as demons and—

'You're giving yourself the "I'll show them! I'll show them all!" pep talk, aren't you?' drawled Loiter.

61

'Shut up.' I peered up at him. 'How did you…?'

'Clenched fists, gritted teeth, furrowed brow, wild eyes. Classic signs.'

'Very funny. But just you—'

'Wait and see?' His eyes glittered with mirth.

Stupid Loiter. Always cracking me up when I was trying to be fierce. 'You know me too well. I'm afraid I'm going to have to kill you.'

'You can try,' said Loiter, sliding down from his hammock. 'Uncharted 3: Necromancer, or Mass Slaughter 2?'

Jinx picked up a controller with a grin. 'You pick. Either way, you're both going down.'

'It's very hard to stay annoyed at you two,' I said accusingly.

'We are terribly charming,' said Loiter. 'Oh but first tell me – what exactly is this opening trial going to involve? I'm curious. Lilith isn't exactly known for fair fights.'

I shrugged. 'All I know is it's taking place somewhere called the Evil Eyrie.'

He raised an eyebrow. 'Is it now? Let me tell you something about the Eyrie…'

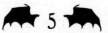 5

# How Not to Make an Omelette

TOMMY

ON MOANDAY MORNING, I tumbled out of bed, opened my bedroom window and took a deep breath of Hellish air. I never got tired of the view. Golden spires and weather vanes in the shape of serpents and vultures glittered in the swirling emerald mist, and swooping demons pulled passengers in rickshaws above the rooftops and curling red minarets. There was no rain in Hell, which was nice, but no sun either – although it still somehow got darker at night, which I couldn't quite figure out. I yawned contentedly, sat at the desk and started to write.

## A GUIDE TO LUCIFER'S PALACE

· Darkangel Palace has hundreds of rooms. Morning rooms and evening rooms and dungeons and libraries and kitchens and art galleries. There's a special room just for breakfast, for Heaven's sake. If I searched hard enough I could probably find an elevenses room.

· My bedroom is in a TURRET. How cool is that? It's all stone and wood and circular and everything.

· Jinx's room is in the next turret along, joined by a covered bridge. It's pretty much the same as mine, except there are no spikemoths fluttering round my rafters (I made sure of that) and he got the Slaystation (he made sure of that).

· Hell has the best showers ever, because the water's pumped up straight from the fiery moat.

· The hairdryer is a little stone dragon on my bedroom wall. He's too old to breathe fire any more, but he does hot air pretty well. Even if you do end up smelling a bit smoky.

· My bedroom alone is bigger than the trailer I lived in on Earth.

· Basically, I'm living the life of Riley. Whoever she was.

· So I should be happy, shouldn't I?

Or rather the problem was that I *was* happy. I loved it here. But an evil little voice in the back of my mind kept telling me it was too good to be true, which was why the thought of Persephone coming back tied my stomach in knots. *'Just wait and see how things change when she gets back'* – that's what Jinx had said. But what would become of me if she didn't want me? If she kicked me out?

Beyond the towering city walls, the snow-covered plains of The Fields of the Damned sparkled maliciously at me. I shivered at the memory of being out there, living in a shack surrounded by snow and ice, chilled to the bone, soldiers marching through, beating Boneheads for no reason. The thought of having to go back terrified me. I couldn't, I just couldn't.

Ugh. I crumpled up the paper and stuffed it back in the drawer. Stupid brain.

Everything would be *fine*. I'd just do well in the contest – I was a tiny ninja girl, how hard could it be? – and Persephone would see I was awesome and everything would be all right. I needed to stop thinking so much. Thinking was clearly bad. Grown-ups thought too much and that was why they got wrinkly. I was twelve years old and I was going to enjoy my afterlife and no one could stop me. I went off to get in the shower.

By the time the hour of the contest rolled around, I was tingly with excitement. I'd show all those sneery demons what a Bonehead could do. Even better, I had a brilliant plan, at least for the first trial. OK, it was Loiter's brilliant plan. Still.

I knocked on Jinx's door but there was no reply. Probably hiding, the big wuss. Whatever. I'd show him I could do this without his help too. I skipped down the steps – I mean, strode, in a kickass, warrior-like way – and out of the palace, over the bridge across the fiery moat.

I hailed a rickshaw outside the palace gates and asked to go to the Evil Eyrie. I settled into the rough wooden seat as the red-skinned demon flapped hard and lifted us up into the air. We soared over the city, high above the hubbub and the scurrying figures below. The skies above Pandemonium were bright green today, swirling like the Northern Lights. There didn't exactly seem to be seasons in Hell, at least not inside the city, but the sky changed colour over the months. Summer had been oranges and reds, like flowing lava; autumn, apparently, was green – sometimes as dark as the deepest, scariest forest, sometimes as cheerful as a jelly at a birthday party.

It was going to be a good day. I just knew it.

Soon, I spotted the Eyrie thrusting up into the sky. It looked like a fat Cleopatra's Needle – tall and flat and squared off – but it was made of the same smooth, red, marble-like material as most of the rest of the city, which made it look like a bloody dagger. Lovely. I hoped we weren't going to have to climb it; I didn't see that ending well.

As we drew closer, I could make out dozens of skeletal birds with no flesh on their bones and dusty sockets for eyes, whooping and cawing around the roof of the tower. Well, no one had said this was going to be fun, exactly. Exciting, though. An adventure, I told myself. Jinx had explained that the birds did have some proper Latin name, but they looked like zombie eagles so everyone just called them zeegles. I thought about the trouble I'd had with a bunch of two-headed gamrins trying to peck me to death before. My heart beat faster and my palms started to sweat. It would be fine, though. Totally. I had a plan. *If Loiter guessed right about the trial,* muttered a voice in the back of my mind.

I couldn't make out Lilith, but six or seven slimy-looking fiends were huddled beside the Eyrie, and a large crowd of demon school kids was gathered in the courtyard to the front. Wow. I hadn't realised Lilith's challenge would be quite so popular. There must have been over a hundred little horned kids milling about. One of them was even holding up a banner – a banner that read *Crack Skulls, Tommy!!!* Wait, what?

The taxi driver dropped me off and I took a closer look. It wasn't any old demon holding the sign, of course. It was the only one with bright blue eyes. I shook my head. Jinx may have been the literal spawn of Satan, but he was also nice. I jogged over to him.

'Cool banner,' I mumbled, all thoughts of *I'll show you* fading away.

He punched me on the arm. 'Hey, just 'cos I'm not crazy enough to take part doesn't mean I can't cheer you to an early death.'

'Thanks. I think.'

'Also I'm stealthily spying on Lilith.'

I looked up at the huge banner and smirked. 'Very stealth.'

There was a loud trumpet blast. The group of fiends gathered on the steps of the Eyrie parted, and Lilith appeared in a rush of blue hellfire.

'Show-off,' muttered Jinx.

'How delightful to see so many participants!' she said

with a slick smile. She paused and scanned the crowd, and her yellow eyes alighted on Jinx's banner. Her smile faltered for a second. Great. What had I done? I hadn't even tried anything yet.

'Some of the smarter among you may have already guessed at your task for today.' She twisted slightly and pointed up at the Eyrie. 'But believe me, it won't be as easy as it looks. Your first trial is this: make your way to the top of the tower by any means available – and bring back a zeegle egg. However, once you are up in the air, you are not to return to ground without an egg. To do so will result in disqualification.'

I did a silent fist-pump. Exactly what Loiter had thought it would be.

'There's nothing much at the Eyrie apart from a bunch of birds,' he'd told me the night before. 'Judging by my extensive knowledge of video games, I bet Lilith will have you try to steal one of their eggs from the roof.'

'But I can't fly!' I'd wailed.

'Quite. An unfortunate flaw in the human design. Luckily, I have a cunning plan…'

I turned back to Lilith. 'Zeegle mothers are notoriously fierce in protecting their offspring, so do watch out,' she continued. Her smile went up a notch. 'It would be such a pity if anyone were to die on the first day.'

She was *so* kickass. OK, and possibly quite evil too. Although I wondered why was she making such a big deal out of the danger. It was almost like she was trying to put people off.

'Participants to the front, please!' squeaked a fiend, the one with the unfortunate ratty comb-over. Dozens of demon kids separated themselves from cooing parents and cheering friends and stepped to the front of the courtyard.

'Here goes nothing,' I mumbled to Jinx.

'You can do it,' he said. 'Just remember you're the kid who argued with an angel.'

I smirked at the memory.

Lilith cleared her throat, which sounded like a bat gargling. 'On your marks, get set…fly!'

There was a whooshing sound like an aeroplane taking off, and a hundred demon kids rose into the sky as one. I waited till they'd all gone, then walked casually across the courtyard to the bottom of the Eyrie. There was laughter from the crowd.

'Stupid Bonehead can't fly!' stage-whispered someone.

'Thinks she can climb up!' another said, snickering.

Almost instantly, the swooshing above turned into a maelstrom of punching and swearing. Black wings crashed

70

against one another and shouts and screams echoed across the courtyard. Three boys and a girl fell out of the sky and landed in a nearby thorn bush with thuds.

'Disqualified!' squealed a fiend.

The crowd began to roar for their favourites.

I marched on up the steps and knocked on the door. There was a rattling of keys and it swung open.

'Hey! Is that allowed? I thought that door was supposed to be locked?' I heard someone shout as I slipped in and the door creaked shut behind me.

'Hello, sir,' I said, to the Zeegle Meister.

'Hello, Miss Tomasina, pleased to meet you.'

The Zeegle Meister was a tall, thin demon whose bones creaked as he walked, just like his beloved birds. Appropriately, he had the brown feathered head and round eyes of a barn owl. We were in a square room filled with piles of paper and pens and ink. Above us, a stone staircase spiralled high up into the air. Thuds and yells came from outside.

'Any friend of Loiter is a friend of mine,' continued the meister, parting his beak into what I hoped was a smile. 'Come with me.'

I stepped over a large trapdoor, wondering what lay beneath it, then followed him up the stairs until we came to

another room about halfway up. This one was stuffed full of cabinets neatly labelled with different destinations. Loiter had explained that the Eyrie was the telecommunications tower of Pandemonium. Letters and parcels came in and out every day, and were never lost. Apparently it was tough to fight off a zeegle to steal their post. Since Loiter was incorrigibly lazy – literally – he used the Zeegle Post more than anyone. Anything to avoid having to get out of bed and actually go somewhere himself.

'I'm his best customer,' he'd told me. 'I'm pretty sure the

meister would be happy to do me a favour.'

To my relief, he'd clearly been right. The meister picked up a small slatted wooden box and presented it to me. 'One zeegle egg, fresh today,' he said, doing his odd beak-smile.

I handed him the envelope Loiter had given me and a ten-demonius note. 'Thank you. One letter for a village in England called Lovecraft, from Loiter.'

He took the letter then led me back downstairs. My curiosity got the better of me. 'What's down there?' I asked, pointing at the trapdoor.

'A door to a million different worlds,' he said.

I rolled my eyes. 'I'm not a kid, you know, there's no need to tease me.'

His wing feathers fluttered slightly, and I realised he was offended. 'I am not,' he said. 'Do you not know about The Waiting Room?'

I tried to remember. 'Jinx told me…I know – it's the place where demons go through to Earth. I think.'

'Correct. In The Waiting Room demons may travel to any time and place on Earth. Well, here in my humble abode I have a small Waiting Room of my own, only it's strictly for the birds.'

'Ohhh,' I said. 'So they can deliver letters to anywhere? That's really cool.'

He twitched his beak. 'It is rather. Now, haven't you got a competition of some sort to win?'

'Oh. Yes. Sorry. Thanks again.'

He unlocked the door, nodded kindly, and I slipped out. Well, that had been ridiculously easy.

Outside it looked like someone had been trying to make an omelette and failing badly. The courtyard was covered in smashed eggs, and bruised kids sulking and wailing. A handful of demons had made it back and were offering up their eggs to Lilith, who nodded coolly down at them whilst a fiend took down their names. Above me, dozens more continued to swoop and fight. I'd thought all this carnage would delight Miss Supervillainess, but she looked like she could barely conceal her rage. I wondered what she'd thought was going to happen. Was she unimpressed?

Whatever. I walked up to her, held up the box, and opened it smugly to reveal one shining black zeegle egg.

She raised an eyebrow at me. 'Bribed the zeegle meister, did we?'

I shrugged. Was I going to get in trouble? I thought suddenly about the humans she'd turned into mice. My palms started to sweat again.

'Quiet!' she shrieked, all of a sudden.

The crowd's roar dulled to a soft whisper.

'This,' she said, pointing at me, 'is how you use your brains. Excellent work, young lady, excellent!' There was still a burning at the back of her eyes, but for a moment I forgot it in the warm glow of praise.

'Woo hoo!' yelled Jinx. 'Go, Tommy!'

I grinned and mentally patted myself on the back for such a cunning plan. Piece of cake.

Then the box holding the egg began to quiver. A crack came from it…and a tiny skeletal head covered in grey slime popped out of the shell.

'What the…?'

I hurriedly put the box down.

All the demon kids who'd completed the task stared at me. None of their eggs had hatched. Oh, *badgers*.

The tiny baby zeegle shook off the remains of the shell, clawed its way up my leg and rubbed his beak against my arm. Then it squawked, squawking something that sounded disturbingly like 'Mama!'

Everyone hooted with laughter.

'Hey, Bonehead, looks like you've made a friend,' said a voice behind me.

'Aw, you'll be a lovely mum!' guffawed a weasel-faced boy.

I felt my cheeks go red. I quickly gave Lilith my name,

and she handed me an envelope with *Trial Two* inscribed on the front. Then I took the baby bird and placed it gently on the ground. 'Stay!' I said, and dashed off towards the crowd. But baby bird was having none of it. 'Mama!' it squeaked, more clearly this time.

I reached Jinx, who was trying very hard not to laugh but failing miserably.

'Come on, let's get out of here,' I said, 'I've completed the trial.'

But Jinx just cracked up and pointed behind me. The

zeegle was pelting across the yard towards me on its little legs, its wings flapping uselessly but enthusiastically.

Jinx gave me puppy eyes.

'Oh no. No way. I am not keeping that thing.'

But *that thing* had caught up with me now. It clawed its way up my leg and settled into my hoody pocket with a satisfied caw.

I threw my hands in the air. 'Fine! For now. But only for now. Sparky wouldn't like it, for starters.'

Jinx nodded, eyes swimming with laughter, and dragged me out of the courtyard.

'I am going to *kill* Loiter,' I growled.

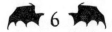

# The Writing on the Wall

JINX

TOMMY STORMED OFF across the courtyard, adoring cawing noises coming from her pocket. I wiped away tears of laughter and hurried after her.

We left the Eyrie courtyard and came out into a wide street bustling with demons shopping and chatting and haggling. A delicious smell of roasting meat wafted from a tiny café called Dreadful. For a second I lost Tommy in the crowd of pointy horns. I dashed after her.

'Tommy, *wait*. Where are you going?'

'Home.' She stuck her bottom lip out. 'I couldn't just have my moment of glory, could I? Something had to come along and make me look like an idiot Bonehead in front of everyone. Just when I was doing so well.'

'Hey, come on, it was funny, that was all. You didn't look like an idiot. I thought it was really clever how you cheated to get the egg. All the demon kids were just jealous a human outfoxed them. They'll be nursing their egos for days.'

She sighed.

'And you're still in the contest! That's the main thing.' I wracked my brains to think of something to take her mind off the tiny bird squawking in her coat. 'Oh, and Lilith!'

She looked up. 'Did you find something out?'

'Not exactly, but I did notice something odd. She looked really angry. Dunno what that was about.'

'I noticed that too.'

'See. I bet it means I was right. She's angry about Some Secret Thing.'

'Could be.'

'Anyway, you keep adventuring and I'll keep investigating.' Then I had an idea. 'Hang on, I know what we can do! Follow me.'

'What we can do about what?'

'Well, it's true that a sharp-clawed zombie eagle and an electrical baby octopus might not make the best of friends.' The zeegle squeaked indignantly at me. 'But I bet Loiter wouldn't mind his own personal messenger. Let's go and ask him.'

Her face brightened. 'Jinx D'Evil, you are a prince. I mean, you *are* a prince, but...'

'I know.' I strode off, but Tommy grabbed my arm. 'The palace is that way.'

'Loiter'll be at home.'

'I thought he lived in the palace. He's always in your room.'

I headed off down the street. 'That's 'cos he's usually hiding from the six other Deadly Sins patrons, or anyone else trying to get him to go to Earth and do some work. He has a house on the edge of the Pale Pastures – it's not far from here.'

'Huh. I suppose he would have a house, being a grown-up and all. Not that he acts like it half the time. Which is one of the things I like about him.'

Jinx smiled. 'Me too.'

We ducked down an alleyway, past an electronics shop called Evil Edna's, its window flickering with dozens of TVs all tuned to a horror film showing a girl hiding under a bed. We stopped for a second to watch, then I happened to look up and my stomach dropped. I yanked Tommy's arm. 'Come on, let's not hang around here.'

'Why? Is this a dodgy part of town or somethi—' Then she saw it too.

Scrawled on the wall in red spray paint were the words 'DEATH TO ALL BONEHEADS'.

I waved my hand vaguely. 'Stupid graffiti, ignore it. Doesn't make any sense, anyway, Boneheads are already dead.'

Tommy looked distinctly queasy.

We hurried off and sped through two more alleys then up a long, narrow street lined with jewellery shops filled with glittering diamond pentagrams and rubies in the shape of devilish heads. Each time someone jostled Tommy, she jumped. I wanted to tell her not to worry, that she wasn't in any danger. But the truth was, I didn't know. Maybe it was just nothing. But maybe...

'Are we there yet?' she fake-whined.

'Nearly.' I pointed off to the right. 'The Pale Pastures are at the end of that road.'

We turned into a quiet avenue called Columbus Street and passed an ironmonger cheerfully displaying thumbscrews and guillotines beside light bulbs and picture hooks. I froze. There was more graffiti. But this was a drawing, not words – a drawing of a demon holding up a decapitated head. A decapitated head with freckles, and blonde plaits that stuck out either side, just like Tommy.

Tommy paled. 'I think I'm going to throw up.'

I felt a bit like I might too. 'I'm so sorry, I'd never have brought you through here if... I had no idea.' I'd joked about demons hating Boneheads, but I hadn't thought anyone would actually dare to do anything to Tommy – not since she was under Dad's protection. 'Come on, we're nearly there. We can get a rickshaw back to the palace after.'

She nodded, and scurried on. At last the avenue came out, not onto another street or square, but onto fields, and I breathed a sigh of relief.

'Huh?' said Tommy.

'What?'

'I thought there were no flowers and stuff in Hell?'

'There aren't. This is muttergrass, see?'

Before us stretched a wide pasture covered in waving grey grass that seemed to whisper in the wind, dotted with animals a little like Earthly Highland cows, horned and shaggy, but bright yellow, and twice as big.

Tommy stared. 'What are *those*?'

'Dreadbeasts. We have to get our food from somewhere, remember?'

Her hand flew to her mouth. 'That's what I've been eating?'

'Yup.' I headed across the muttergrass and Tommy followed me warily.

'That one's looking at us.' She waved at a group of a dozen dreadbeasts grazing peacefully a hundred feet from us. 'They don't fool me with their big doe eyes.'

I laughed. 'Dreadbeasts wouldn't hurt a fly, don't be silly.' I pointed to the other side of the field. 'Look, there's Loiter's house.'

Her eyes grew even wider. On the far side of the pastures, teetering alone against the city walls, stood one of the most fantastical houses in the city, and that was saying a lot in Pandemonium, with its glowing marble and magical buildings that had sprung up clean out of the ground. It was true that Loiter's home was not what I'd imagined back before I'd first seen it. It was neither a tree nor a pigsty.

Instead it was an overgrown helter-skelter. A circular wooden tower thrust up into the swirling sky, painted in green and white stripes with a slide round the outside encased in glass. The slide opened onto each floor and finished by disappearing into the house to the left of a bright red front door. There were no windows above the second floor, and on the small flat rooftop a hammock was strung between two pillars carved in the shape of sloths.

Tommy seemed to forget about weird yellow hellbeasts and scary graffiti. 'That is so cool. And it's so...new-looking. I mean, I was kind of expecting...'

'A falling-down old shack? Loiter has a bit of help around the house, that's why it's so pristine. You'll see.'

We plunged on through the grass. Tommy stopped abruptly and I almost ran into her. 'Did you feel that?' she said.

'Feel what?'

'The ground, it...'

The ground shook.

'It did *that*. Do you have earthquakes in Hell?'

'No.'

It shook again, and a distant rumbling echoed through the air. I looked back the way we'd come and all the air was sucked out of my lungs.

The dozen dreadbeasts were no longer peacefully grazing. Instead they were stampeding straight at us in an extremely unpeaceful manner.

'Run!'

I spun round and hurtled through the pasture, Tommy beside me. The rumbling grew louder and louder. Trampled to death by dreadbeasts. Well, that was new. The muttergrass scratched at me as I flew on towards Loiter's house. In front of it was a wooden fence that encircled the field. Surely they wouldn't be able to get past that? I threw a glance over my shoulder. Several tons of furry yellow monsters were gaining on us, and they didn't look happy. Never mind a fence, they looked like they could break down the Celestial Wall. *And* I was getting a stitch.

Tommy hurtled over the boundary fence and I followed.

We slammed through Loiter's front door and hurled it shut behind us.

'Loiter!' I yelled. 'Loiter! Bit of a problem!'

Tommy ran to the window. 'They've stopped. They've stayed behind the fence. They still look like someone insulted their mothers, though.'

The second floor of the tower shook faintly. There was a crashing noise and a shaggy demon in a bedraggled pink bathrobe tumbled out of the slide in front of us.

'I say, bit of a rude awakening, chaps,' grumbled Loiter.

'We were being attacked!' I said.

'By those giant yellow monsters!' said Tommy, pointing angrily out of the window.

'You were what?' He ambled up and pressed his furry nose to the window pane. 'The dreadbeasts? Don't be silly, they're harmless.'

At this point Tommy lost her temper a tiny bit. 'Why does everyone keep saying hellbeasts are harmless when all they ever do is try to murder me to death?' she wailed.

Loiter looked taken aback.

I puffed out my cheeks. 'I know they're usually harmless, Loiter, don't you think I know that? But they weren't just now. They tried to trample us!'

'Or possibly eat us,' added Tommy, brow creased with anger.

'Or possibly eat us.'

'Huh. My apologies, I believe you, of course. But that is most curious behaviour.' He threw open the front door and loped out.

'What are you doing?' said Tommy. 'They might still be dangerous!'

We both hovered in the doorway, hardly daring to breathe, as Loiter strolled nonchalantly up to the fence.

'Fence is enchanted,' he said. 'They can't get out. Made

sure of it after one wandered into my garden and ate all my grimberries.' He held his hands against the fence and muttered a few words. 'There. Spell renewed. Just in case.'

The dreadbeasts clustered by the fence, however, hadn't taken the hint. They pressed their yellow shaggy noses up against the wooden bars of their cage, mooing angrily.

Loiter tilted his head. 'Very curious behaviour indeed. Perhaps one got bitten by a spikemoth and set the others off. I shouldn't worry about it.'

Tommy growled and muttered to herself. 'Don't worry about it – ten-ton yellow monsters are trying to eat you but, oh no, that's just another day in Hell.'

Loiter came back inside and shut the front door behind him. 'You two look like you could do with a nice mug of hot chocolate.'

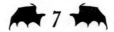

# The Laziest House in the World

### JINX

LOITER AMBLED AROUND the kitchen, plucking packets and mugs from shelves, still dressed in his crumpled pink dressing gown.

'So he *does* wear clothes sometimes,' whispered Tommy.

Loiter poured some milk into a pan. 'So! How did the contest go?'

I looked at the tiny head peeking out of Tommy's pocket. 'Ah. That's what we were coming to talk to you about. Before we nearly got eaten by our food.'

Tommy squeaked as a small shape darted across the floor. 'What are *those*?'

Now that the commotion had died down, Loiter's circular living room was dotted with brown fluffy creatures that rolled this way and that like curled-up hedgehogs.

'Oh, they're my dibbles,' said Loiter. 'Wonderful creatures, brilliant at cleaning. Don't worry, they don't bite.'

Tommy took a very deep breath and just glared at us both.

'Oi, you lot, shoo!' said Loiter.

The dibbles squeaked and disappeared one by one through the catflap.

'Told you Loiter had help,' I said.

'Quite, quite,' said Loiter. 'I can't be expected to do *housework*.' He mock-shuddered.

'How come you don't have any windows on the top floor?' asked Tommy.

'Bedrooms are up there. Don't need any pesky daylight waking me up.'

I wandered around the lounge. Everything was set up exactly as you'd imagine for the Patron Demon of Sloth. There was a fridge by the sofa, so Loiter didn't have to bother going to the kitchen, which was all of ten feet away. Above the stove, a hammock swayed from the rafters.

'Has he got a bed in every room?' asked Tommy.

'Of course. I mean, he has proper bedrooms upstairs, but in case he can't be bothered to go all that way...'

Tommy pointed at a door in a fat wooden pillar in the middle of the lounge. Beside the door was a glowing red button marked with an arrow. 'In case he hasn't got the energy to use the *lift*?' she said incredulously.

'I think you're forgetting that Loiter is the literal embodiment of laziness.'

'Wow. How come I've never seen dibbles before?' said Tommy.

'Most demons prefer to use serfs for their cooking and cleaning,' said Loiter over his shoulder. 'But I don't like having anyone else in my house. They always wake me up. Terribly irritating.' He gestured to two big cosy yellow sofas in the middle of the room. 'Do have a seat.' I flopped onto a chair while Tommy looked around, her face alight with curiosity. White wooden bookcases encircled the room, each shelf studded with rows of buttons. Tommy prodded one and took a hurried step backwards as the shelf before her spun round, revealing yet more books behind it. 'The bookcases are *motorised*?'

'Yeah. Loiter has a study upstairs, and if he wants a book…look, I'll show you. Wait a sec.' I jumped up, got into the lift, zoomed up one whole floor, and tapped a few keys on Loiter's computer. Then I slid back downstairs in the slide, arriving just as a book fell off a bookcase with a click and a whirr and landed neatly in a little cart.

Tommy looked up and her mouth fell open. Above us the cart carrying the book sped along a Scalextric track, which wound around the ceiling above our heads like a black plastic spider's web. The cart zoomed through the rafters, up a ramp that twirled round and round like a spiral staircase, then disappeared through a hole in the ceiling.

There was a muffled thud from overhead. 'That's the book landing on the desk in Loiter's study.'

Tommy gasped. 'That is *awesome*. We need one of those for our floor in the palace. We could pass notes up and down the corridor.'

'That's actually a pretty good idea.'

'Aren't my ideas always?'

I narrowed my eyes and mimicked her voice. '*Let's go through the Frozen Forest!*' I said pointedly.

She narrowed her eyes right back at me. 'Carnivorous carousel horses.'

'Yeah, all right, call it even.'

Loiter came out of the kitchen and handed us each a steaming mug.

Tommy took hers and peered out of the window at the fields beyond. 'We really eat those things?'

'Indeed,' said Loiter. 'Main source of meat in Pandemonium. We do bring in things from Earth occasionally, but they're very rare and expensive. There are also pikbeasts – they're smaller and taste a bit like your

Earth venison. Oh, and mungbeasts, which we use for fabric to make clothes, and for milk. Similar to sheep, except they have two heads.'

'I think I'll give dreadburgers a miss after today,' I said.

Loiter sank into an armchair and Tommy sat down on one of the yellow sofas. The sofa gave out a groan like an unhappy elephant and she jumped straight back up again.

'What was *that*?'

Loiter waved his hand. 'Oh, don't worry, he does that. Gets grumpy sometimes. Oliver, settle down!'

Tommy backed away. 'Your sofa...is called Oliver? What is it?'

'A sofa. Oliver has ideas above his standing, that's all. Used to be a dreadbeast, misses the pastures. Your glory days are over, Oliver, get over it!' Loiter growled.

'That's why I'm sitting over here,' I whispered.

Tommy's eyes widened and she perched on a small wooden chair instead.

Loiter clapped his hands together. 'So, how did it go? Old Zeegy remember me, did he?'

'He did, thank you. Your help was really...helpful.' Tommy pulled the baby zeegle from her pocket. 'Except for one small problem.'

'Oh dear, egg hatch on you, did it?'

The baby zeegle squawked 'Mama!' and rubbed his beak against Tommy's palm.

I smothered a snort.

She looked daggers at us both. 'Yes. You didn't warn me about that part.'

Loiter raised an eyebrow. 'Did all the eggs hatch, then,' he asked, 'for everyone?'

Tommy raised her eyes to the ceiling. 'No,' she admitted.

'Interesting. Perhaps zeegles have a soft spot for humans. Or just for you.'

Tommy frowned. 'Just what I need. A pet that'll remind everyone how human I am. Please, Loiter, will you look after it for me? If it follows me around everywhere – everyone will laugh at me.'

'I don't see why. Pretty fierce pet to have.'

'It calls me *Mama*.'

Loiter chuckled. 'Fine, fine. Maybe I can train it to send messages for me. Give it here. Has it got a name?'

Tommy's shoulders slumped in relief. 'Thank you. And no, no name yet.'

Loiter turned the tiny skeleton bird upside down gently. 'A girl. All right, let's call you...Loretta.'

I spat a mouthful of hot chocolate across the room.

'You don't think Loretta suits her?' asked Loiter. 'You may be right. I always was more of a Dolly Parton fan anyway. Dolly, welcome to your new home.'

The bird squinted suspiciously at Loiter. Then she rubbed her beak gently against Loiter's paw, as though she were testing him out. 'Mama?' she said.

Loiter broke into a grin. 'Yes, I'm your new mama,' he said. 'And you're going to be trained to be my lickle slave and fly everywhere dropping off messages for me,' he continued in a baby voice.

Tommy grinned. 'Thanks, Loiter, I owe you one.'

'Ooh, never say that to a demon,' said Loiter, suddenly looking devilish. 'You don't know what I might ask you to do in return.' He plucked a discarded top hat from a bookcase and announced to Dolly that it would be her new bed.

'Now, let's see, you need some bedding. I know, muttergrass!' He ambled outside.

'So when's the next trial?' I asked Tommy.

'Tomorrow. Are you sure you don't want to come and keep me company? I don't want to accidentally pick up any more pets.'

'Sorry, you can keep your death-defying idea of fun to yourself. I don't know if you noticed but there was carnage out there today.'

Tommy pouted. Then a gleam appeared in her eyes. 'If you're not busy tomorrow, would you go to the library for me? To see if you can find anything out about Pandora?'

'We could go now, if you wanted?'

She looked outside at the darkening sky and wrinkled her freckled nose. 'Not that I'm scared or anything, *obviously*, but I'm not dying to wander round the city after nightfall,

95

what with the graffiti and rampaging yellow monsters.'

'Oh.' Fair enough. And I did owe her. 'OK, I'll go.'

'Thanks.'

Loiter came back in and settled Dolly into her new grass-filled top-hat bed. The little bird cheeped happily and drifted off to sleep.

'So,' I said to Loiter, 'what—'

Loiter vanished into thin air.

Tommy and I stared at the spot where he'd been standing.

'I guess he had to be somewhere in a hurry,' she said.

I frowned. 'Loiter never does *anything* in a hurry.'

'Do you think he's in trouble? Should we do something?'

'I honestly have no idea. Um...let's just wait for a bit.'

'OK.'

We'd been staring at the rug in the middle of the room for ten minutes and I was really beginning to worry when there was a flash of amber light and Loiter popped back into existence.

'Loiter! Are you all right? Where did you go?'

'Hmph,' he said, smoothing down his fur. 'I was summoned. By a human! Can't remember the last time that happened.'

'Not to be cheeky or anything,' said Tommy, 'but why would they summon you? For extra lazy power?'

Loiter threw a sharp claw into the air and she took a step back, but he was only reaching up for a rafter. He hung upside down from the ceiling and took a deep breath. 'Millennia ago, humans used to summon all kinds of demons to do their bidding. But when the Great Library at Alexandria burned, nearly all the scrolls containing the incantations were lost forever. There was a lot more information about how to summon the Devil, and some of the stories were just handed down in folklore, like meeting the Devil at midnight by a crossroads, that kind of thing. So it still happens to Lucifer now and then. But the rest of us...not any more.'

'So what happened just now?' I asked.

Loiter's frown melted into a chuckle. 'Some idiot human got so tangled up in his duvet, he accidentally arranged it in a pentagram. Then he swore quite creatively in Arabic and accidentally used the words needed to summon me. It's not very hard if you know how. Or, apparently, even if you don't.'

Tommy giggled.

'It was quite funny. You should have seen his face. One moment he was half asleep alone in the Cairo Hilton, dreaming about breakfast in bed, next minute he was face to face with an angry sloth. I think he thought he was hallucinating. Anyway, moving on. What's your next trial? Can I help at all?'

Tommy pulled an envelope out of her pocket and tore it open. 'All it says is the second trial takes places at Sharp Point.'

'The military academy? Where your dad wanted to send you?' said Loiter to me.

'Yup. Thank the dark lords he changed his mind about that one. So I guess it'll just be some straightforward fighting test. Hand to hand combat or something. You're good at that.'

Tommy preened. 'Well, we did fight off Dantalion and a whole demon army. How hard can one test be?'

'You might die horribly.'

She stuck her tongue out. '*You* might die horribly in the library. Watch out for bottomless abysses.'

Ah yes. Great. I stood up. 'Anyway, we'd better get going. Loiter, can you get us a rickshaw?' I didn't want to risk any more stampedes.

A few minutes later we were safely ensconced in a cab, high above the Pale Pastures. 'Don't worry about the graffiti,' I said to Tommy. 'I'm sure it's just a couple of idiots. I'll get Dad to sort it out.'

'And the homicidal cows?' she said, frowning down

at the fields below.

'I'm sure it was nothing.' Although I wasn't, not really.

As we flew over Columbus Street I couldn't help but look down at the drawing of the beheaded girl and shudder. But we'd be back to the safety of the palace soon enough, and tomorrow I'd go to Babel to find out more about Pandora. Maybe if everyone knew Tommy was descended from some badass evil queen they'd leave her alone. Everything would be fine. We had the King of Hell on our side, after all. Dad would never let anything bad happen to Tommy.

# When One Door Closes, It's Possible You're Doomed

TOMMY

I YAWNED INTO the bathroom mirror. Dark circles were smudged above my freckles and my hair looked like a haystack some passing pigs had used for a party. My head had been too busy swirling with thoughts of Pandora and Persephone and stampeding hellbeasts to get much sleep. It was Tauntday, which meant I only had three days left before the Queen of the Damned returned home. Maybe I needed to summon Loiter for sleep tips. Or How to Get On the Good Side of Evil Queens tips.

Unlike with the Evil Eyrie egg party, none of us could guess what the second trial was going to be, so I was going to have to wing it this time. I threw on some clothes and gave Sparky a stern look.

'No setting fire to things while I'm out, OK?'

He ignored me and continued snoring on the windowsill, blowing out little sparks with each breath.

I stuck my head out of the window and spotted Grrr and Argg. '⚑🔮👁👁 🐾🔮🐉 👁🔮💀👹 💀☀ 💀🐾💀📖🔮👁👁 🔮☀ ⊂🔮💀 ➲→🔮🔮📖 🔱🔮← 🏠💀 ' I asked.

Grrr tossed his stone lion's mane and agreed to watch over Sparky.

I turned to go… At which point Sparky opened both eyes, threw out a stream of sparks, and set fire to the curtains.

'Sparky! If you wanted to come you could've just said so.'

I picked up a rug and smacked the curtains until they were forlorn and blackened, but non-flaming.

'⊂🔮 📖💀 🔱💀🔮← 🔮💀 👁👹☀ ⊂ ⊂👹🔮👁👁 ' said Arrg.

'I know he can't talk but…' I growled at the baby shocktopus and slid him into my hoody pouch. Maybe he'd come in useful, anyway. I went along the covered bridge, but Jinx wasn't in his room. Perhaps he was already waiting for me with a banner – or even better, in the library, finding out all about my kickass ancestor. I trudged off down the stairs and out of the palace, rubbing my eyes sleepily.

On the other side of the moat, I was greeted by a coach full of hollering demon kids. I climbed up the steps and the hollering stopped.

'Bonehead,' spat a voice. Another joined in, then another. I ignored them and headed for the back of the bus, but tripped over someone's outstretched foot and landed hard on my knee. Two red-skinned boys cackled. I got up and kicked the nearest one hard in the shin. He howled.

'Just because I'm human, don't think you can mess with me,' I hissed, stomping off to sit by myself near the back. I added an extra item to my To Do List.

(a) Fit in as well as any demon before Persephone comes back

(b) Find out more about Pandora

(c) Crush those idiot boys in the contest. Dorkfaces

A few minutes later the bus was full and we rumbled off through the city. I chewed my bottom lip nervously, wondering again what this trial would be. I had to do well. I had to prove to Persephone and the stupid demon graffiti artists that I belonged here.

I counted around forty chattering kids on the bus – forty kids who'd survived the first trial, out of over a hundred. At this rate we'd be down to zero before we even made the final test. No one had died yet, despite Lilith's warnings, but nine entrants had ended up in hospital with cracked horns and torn wings. Maybe *that* was what Lilith was up to. Maybe she just didn't like kids. I made a mental note to tell Jinx.

The gates of Sharp Point reared up before us – literally, as they had mechanical dragons carved into them that flapped their wings up and over the bus. Cool. We swung into a large courtyard. The academy was made of slick, blood-red marble like most of the city, but the main building before us was studded with extremely pointed turrets that looked like they might put your eye out if you flew by too closely.

As we got off the bus, several cars and rickshaws and a green minibus parked behind us, and gaggles of parents and friends got out. I craned my neck for Jinx but couldn't see him.

The fiends shepherded us into the school, along a hallway and into a large vaulted chamber which smelled vaguely of sweaty socks. I spun round. Every inch of the walls and ceiling were covered in murals of battles, anguished faces and spurting blood everywhere like a scene from a gangster movie. Glass cabinets down the left-hand side of the room held enough weapons to stop a zombie apocalypse, and two doors off to the right were marked 'Girls" and 'Boys' Changing Rooms'. So that was where the sweaty sock smell was coming from. We were in the Sharp Point training room. It *was* hand-to-hand combat today. Well, all right. That I could do. I smiled at the thought of getting my own back on the sneery kids from the bus.

At the top of the chamber the fiends gathered in front of two sturdy steel doors. The fiend with the comb-over stood off to one side, staring vaguely out of the window, not paying attention. Maybe he wasn't in charge for this trial. The crowd of kids shoved me forward until I was a few feet away, and I saw that the right-hand door was marked 'Exit'. The left-hand door had a frame for a plaque, but it was empty. Above us on the wall were dozens of plaques, but I couldn't see what they had written on them from where I was standing.

A tinkling laugh rang through the chamber. I turned to see Lilith slink in – a happy, beaming Lilith, laughing flirtatiously at something the big, red-skinned demon next to her was saying. *Lucifer.*

'Your Badness?'

'Hello, Tommy!' he said. 'Well done for getting this far. Thought I'd come and see what all the excitement was about. Don't mind, do you?'

'Of course not.' But I couldn't help noticing Lilith's hand resting on Lucifer's arm. Uh oh. Maybe that was it. Maybe she was trying to get Jinx's dad back. Jinx was so not going to be happy about that. Perhaps I'd better not say anything. I glared at the back of her head, willing her to remove her hand. Eventually, she did.

She turned to the waiting crowd. 'So, today is the second physical trial.' The words fell from her lips like smooth pebbles, the usual hiss gone. 'But unlike the first, today you will choose your own fate.' She flicked a finger at the blank door in the back wall. 'Behind this door are numerous challenges based upon different sins. Once inside your room, you must make it out in one piece. That is all.' She pointed to the second door marked 'Exit'. 'Succeed and you will come out through this door. If you have not appeared after an hour, someone will come to fetch you, and you will be disqualified from the tournament. Choose your sin wisely.'

Sins. *Badgers*. Fighting, I knew – sins, not so much. Well, apart from accidentally murdering your uncle.

'Questions?' purred Lilith.

The boy I'd kicked stuck his hand up. 'So do we do this one by one? Seems like that'd take all day.'

'No, my dear impatient child, you do not do it one by one. The room beyond this is used for hellion training, and may be turned into whatever battlefield or place we need. Queue up, choose your sin, and we will insert the correct plaque in the door. Once the door is shut behind you, the next contestant may enter. They will find a completely different room on the other side. Anything else?'

'Do we get weapons?' asked a grey-faced girl at the front.

'No weapons are to be taken with you. However, once you are inside the room, the appropriate weapons will appear to you. They may not always come in the most obvious guise.'

Great. With my luck I'd have to fend off a kraken with a ping-pong bat.

'You have ten minutes to choose your sin,' said Lilith, 'starting now.'

Lilith, Lucifer and the fiends stood to one side and we all rushed forward and craned our necks up at the wall. In gold letters on small wooden plaques, the dozens of options glared down at us, daring us to pick Fury or Jealousy or Deception. But one plaque right at the bottom caught my eye. Sloth. Of course! That'd be easy. 'Easy' was Loiter's life motto, after all.

There were five pupils ahead of me on the alphabetical list. When the ten minutes were up, a small fiend as naked and wrinkly as a hairless cat announced 'Alisha Allnasty'. The fiend with the comb-over was still standing by the window. He had an oddly dreamy look in his eyes.

A broad-shouldered, red-skinned girl pushed her way to the front.

'Your choice is?' said the fiend.

'Sloth,' replied Alisha.

Gah, she'd pinched my idea.

The fiend reached up, removed the wooden plaque with Sloth on it and slid it into the empty space on the front of the door.

'Good luck, darling!' yelled a female voice from the back of the crowd.

Alisha yanked open the door, presumably to get away from her embarrassing mother as quickly as possible. I peered past her, but the space beyond was pitch black. She took a deep breath and stepped inside. Just before the door swung shut behind her, I heard her scream. I gulped. Apparently Sloth wasn't as safe as it sounded. Sloth equalled sleep, equalled...nightmares? Possibly. Perhaps none of the options were safe.

I scanned the plaques hurriedly, looking for a new choice. Wait, there was one: Vanity didn't exactly sound violent. Maybe I'd have to steal face masks and fake tan from angry supermodels. I could manage that.

The kid up next, a thick-necked boy with muscles bunched under his shirt like boulders, strode to the front. Before the fiend in charge could even say anything, he barked 'Fury!' at him. Show-off. The fiend slid in the plaque into the door with a gleam in his eyes. Thug Boy opened the door and strode straight in, but not before there was a small gasp from the crowd. The room beyond had been on fire.

By the time it was my turn, the anticipation was killing me. When my name was read out I zipped straight to the front of the crowd. Lucifer gave me a quick nod as I walked past. I'd show those demons I was as good as them. The wrinkled fiend opened his mouth to ask me what I'd chosen – and at that moment the exit door on the right hand side of the room flew open. A sobbing, hyperventilating Alisha stumbled out and crashed to the floor. The crowd applauded, but she didn't seem to notice. She flapped her hands around her head like she was fighting off invisible monsters. Her arms were scratched and bleeding.

*Yikes.* My hands twitched, suddenly wishing they were holding a pair of hira-shuriken.

'Your choice?' asked the fiend.

I dragged my eyes away from the sobbing girl and mumbled 'Vanity'. Demons cackled behind me and I straightened my shoulders. On the bright side, whatever hellish nightmare I was stepping into, those morons would have to survive their own version of it too.

The fiend slid the plaque marked 'Vanity' into the door. I took a deep breath, turned the doorknob, and walked through.

# Welcome to the House of Fun

TOMMY

THE DOOR SHUT behind me with a soft click and for a moment a mist hung in the air, obscuring my vision. Maybe the room was still changing itself from the previous participant's challenge. Then the fog evaporated and my eyes bulged out.

That was so not what I'd expected.

I was standing in front of a turnstile. I looked back. The door I'd come through had vanished. Behind me now stood a rickety wooden wall, painted with red and white stripes. The paint was peeling off. Written across it were the words 'Welcome to the Funhouse'. A couple of cans of paint sat on the floor, like someone was planning to do it up. From nearby came the soft tinkling sound of fairground music. I had a flashback to running away from carnivorous carousel horses and my heart started to beat like a drum. I turned back to the entrance. Beside it stood a kiosk, but it was empty. I pushed through the turnstile and it creaked eerily. There was a faint smell of popcorn and sweat and something else, something sweet and sickly, in the air. It was hot too. I pushed my hair out of my eyes.

Opposite me stood a hall of mirrors. I'd never been in one before. The circus I'd worked in hadn't had one, nor the hellish fairground Jinx and I had discovered in the Fields of the Damned. But I'd seen them before...in horror movies. Awesome. At least there were no carousels to be seen. I was about to bite the bullet when I remembered what Lilith had said. 'Once you are inside the room, the appropriate weapons will appear to you.' I stopped. What were appropriate weapons for a hall of mirrors? Make-up? A camera? A selfie-stick?

I took a step back and looked into the empty kiosk again. The glass was so filthy and smudged I could barely see in. I tried the door and it opened easily. A few dried-up pens were scattered on the small counter inside, beside an ancient cash register. An empty coffee cup. Torn popcorn buckets piled on the floor. A smell of rancid butter hanging in the air. Nothing useful.

Then I noticed a drawer beneath the register. I yanked it open and a shriek ripped through the air. I jumped and banged my elbow hard on the counter. I spun round but there was no one there. Another shriek echoed from down the hall and I realised it wasn't a shriek of pain or terror, it was a shriek of laughter.

Really, really creepy laughter.

*Gah.* You know when people say their legs turned to jelly? I understood that now. My knees were definitely wobbly. I gripped the counter and forced myself to think of the Fields of the Damned. I was so not ending up out there again – not ever. I had to impress Persephone somehow, make her like me, make her accept me. And the contest was my best shot. I flipped open my jacket pocket and stroked Sparky a few times to calm my nerves.

'Just a dumb bunch of mirrors. Nothing to be scared of,' I said.

He responded by sending a volt of electricity up my arm.

'Ow! So there *is* something to be scared of? Thanks a lot. You're a great cheerleader.' I zipped my jacket back up.

Then I realised there was one silver lining – no one could see me. I was all alone. Which obviously was bad, but it also meant I could just run through the freaky mirror nightmare and out the other side as fast as I could and no one would ever know I'd been a tiny bit scared... Just a tiny bit. I turned back to the drawer and rattled it open. And found something.

It was an old-fashioned letter opener with a mother-of-pearl handle in the shape of a devil's face, and a sharp, if small, blade. I slipped it into my pocket and rummaged around some more, but only came up with empty chewing gum wrappers, mounds of dust and a worried-looking beetle. Then I remembered the freshly-painted sign. I went out of the kiosk and back past the squeaky turnstile. *Paint*. Hmm. I didn't know what use that would be, but I didn't have much else. I picked up the two tins and set off to meet my doom.

The hallway of mirrors was brightly lit, but the lights flickered, occasionally going out for as much as two or three seconds. I suddenly didn't feel like running. I trod stealthily down the corridor. The laughter had started up again, and this time it didn't stop. It reminded me of the Frozen Forest and I wished Jinx was there with me too. Then I caught something out of the corner of my eye. I whirled round but there was nothing there.

I froze.

There was *nothing* there.

Despite the fact I was looking straight into a mirror. Where was my reflection? The mirror showed an empty hallway. There were no not-at-all-scared blonde girls to be seen. Then I saw something. Up ahead, there were unending full length mirrors lined up next to one another, a parade of them with no wall showing – and something flitted through them. I took the letter opener out of my pocket and kept going. It looked like a dead end, but there was nowhere else to go. I kept on, the lights flickering and the hideous low cackling continuing to ring in my ears.

I reached the end of the corridor and saw with relief that it turned to the right, into another hall of mirrors. Well, at least it wasn't a dead end. But as I turned to continue I suddenly realised the mirror at the end of the first corridor was not empty. There I stood, looking back at myself. I jumped back and my reflection jumped too. Its freckled cheeks were flushed and it was brandishing a letter opener in one hand and two small tins of paint in the other.

Of course it was. *Don't be stupid, Tommy, it's only you.*

And then my reflection grinned – a horrible, dead-eyed grimace – and stepped out of the mirror.

# Staircase to Hell

JINX

THE TOWER OF Babel took up the whole of one side of Nero Plaza, reaching into the green skies like a slightly crumbly wedding cake, circular layer upon circular layer. I peered up at it nervously as the crowds in the square swirled around me, swinging Miss Selfish and Scarehouse shopping bags and chattering about the new Poisoned Apple store. The last time I'd been to the library it had involved bottomless abysses and killer holy water. I wasn't exactly in a hurry to go back. But demons were writing menacing graffiti about Tommy on the city walls, and, possibly not accidentally hellbeasts were chasing us. She was right – maybe if everyone knew she was descended from some famous evil queen they'd leave her alone. I had to try.

I trotted up the wide stone steps and in through a small door cut into the massive wooden double doors at the front. Inside, the hubbub of the plaza instantly faded away, replaced with whispers and dim lighting. The thick stone walls kept it cool and dry inside. Dozens of desks stretched out before me, crammed with horned figures reading and studying. Above my head, the tower soared up more than a hundred feet, spiral staircases linking circular mezzanines stuffed with leather-bound books.

I found a vast map showing the twenty-four different floors, and ran my finger across it, not quite sure what I was looking for. History, maybe? I wondered if that was underground. The library had twelve floors beneath where I was standing. Fiction...Magic...Demon-conjuring... Demonic cookery books...Demonic history...Human history! That'd be it. Fourth floor. Phew. No bottomless abysses up there. Hopefully. I snaked through the desks to the nearest spiral staircase and hurried up it.

When I reached the fourth floor I looked over the balcony and sucked in a breath. The mezzanine was only a few feet wide, and made of the same clanging, ivy-patterned cast iron as the spiral staircases – which meant I could see right down past my feet. My head spun for a second before I remembered I was a demon. Doh. I shook out my wings. I'd been hanging out with Tommy too much.

The stacks radiated out from the mezzanine like hedgehog spikes, and I headed down the nearest one, full of curiosity. Who had Pandora really been? And did it mean

116

anything that Tommy looked like her? A few minutes later I was sittings at a small desk with a pile of books in front of me. I licked my finger and began to read.

An hour later, my bum was numb, my horns were drooping from boredom and I was no nearer finding out anything useful. I thumped *Ancient History Vol XII* onto the pile next to me, on top of *Really Ancient History*, *Evil Humans in Pre-History*, and *Wicked Women We All Want to Be*, and coughed as dust billowed out. They'd all had the same vague story about Pandora and the box. I had one more book in front of me: *Devils in Disguise*, a history of women through the ages. I sighed and ran my finger down the index to Pandora. Page 333.

Pandora of the Northern Tribe was a blacksmith, famed for her skill in forging weapons.

Aha! All the other books (aside from the ones that had the myth about her having been the first human) said she was a queen, or at least a warrior queen. I leant forward on my elbows and scanned the page, suddenly more awake.

Many eons ago in the desert lands of Sumer, a terrified shepherd came to the palace, begging the queen to help him:

117

all his lambs were being born with two heads. The Sorceress Queen of Sumer sent soldiers to investigate and discovered a gateway to Hell in a cave.

Cool, a sorceress queen! Although there wasn't a picture of her, just a grim drawing of soldiers lying dead in front of a cave mouth.

Wanting to prevent anything from getting out, the queen ordered a wall built in front of the cave. But evil continued to seep through. So she commissioned Pandora, who was renowned as a brilliant smith, to create an unbreakable chest to hold any escaped demons or evil spirits. The chest was to be strong enough to withstand the heat of a forest fire, the rage of a tornado, and the weight of an elephant. Pandora tried dozens of different materials, and finally, after many months, succeeded, and delivered the chest to the palace. But only a few weeks later, the chest – now full of evil – was stolen and broken open. Unable to find the culprit, the queen arrested Pandora and sentenced her to death for having failed at making an unbreakable box.

I sat back and stared at the ceiling. Wow. A different story at last.

Beneath the text was a black and white drawing of the box, with all the evils escaping from it. The metalwork on it was plaited like rope. The book didn't say which material Pandora had ended up using. I was pretty sure they hadn't had steel back then. Iron or bronze? Something like that. Beneath the drawing was a caption:

The Unbreakable Box breaks. Even the daggers of the earth could not withstand such evil.

The daggers of the earth? What did that mean?

So Pandora had been framed – or made a scapegoat, anyway. I ran my finger down the page. Except she'd then escaped from prison before she could be put to death, and wisely vanished. And that was the last anyone had ever heard of her. The box had never been seen again, either, although a rumour remained that one evil had not escaped from it, perhaps the greatest evil of all. I looked at the drawing again. War, sickness, fear, hatred, death itself were escaping. What could be worse than death itself? That didn't make any sense.

Then I saw I'd missed the final paragraph of the story.

Unable to punish Pandora for her misdeeds, the Sorceress Queen of Sumer cursed her and her bloodline for all eternity.

Oh, hellfire. Bad sorceress queen. So if Tommy was descended from Pandora – and it seemed pretty likely, given how they were practically twins – she was cursed for all eternity. A curse would certainly explain her bad luck in getting sucked down to Hell along with her uncle, even though she shouldn't have been, even though kids were never sent to Hell.

I tapped my fingers on the table. So now what? Now

being related to Pandora didn't do Tommy any good at all. She wasn't a famous evil queen who was right up there with the best demons. She was an unlucky metalworker, and cursed to boot. Awesome.

Then again, no one but me seemed to know the truth. Loiter had said even Dad didn't remember what happened. So, what if I went to Dad and showed him the painting? Asked him to tell all the other demons – who still thought Pandora was an evil badass – that Tommy was descended from her. Then maybe the horrible demons painting graffiti would stop hating her so much.

It was worth a shot.

I looked at my watch. *Brimstone.* I'd meant to go and cheer Tommy on at her next trial and I was late. I grabbed the book, clanged along the mezzanine to the nearest spiral staircase, and hopped onto it. An alarming creak came from beneath me.

Then the whole staircase came away from the wall.

'Aaargh!'

I clung onto the railing as the steps swung out over the library like a wonky crane. The demons on the ground floor looked up, then panic broke out and everyone started running and yelling.

'Get off there!' yelled a blue-skinned librarian.

Get off? How was I supposed to...oh. Right. I flexed my wings and flapped into the air. Just in time. The staircase screeched like a hungry pterodactyl then crashed onto the floor far below, sending chairs and books flying.

I landed on a desk and gaped at the destruction around me. Nice to see I was still as lucky as ever.

Two furious-looking librarians were storming over to me.

*Ulp.* I ducked into the fleeing crowd and made my escape.

It wasn't till I was halfway back to the palace that I realised my hands were as empty as when I'd arrived. I'd lost the book.

# Who's the Scared-est of Them All?

TOMMY

I SCREECHED SO high Bruce could've heard me, and bolted down the hall of mirrors – which now kindly decided to work, so I could see myself and the mirror creature following fast on my heels.

*Vanity,* I thought, *whose stupid idea was that?*

A red door loomed at the end of the corridor. The way out! I crashed through it and landed on my knees, panting, head hung in relief. Silence.

Why was there silence?

I lifted my head and swallowed a scream.

I was not back in the training hall at Sharp Point. Instead I was in a circular room, with more mirrors surrounding me on every surface. All at once the fairground music blasted out, so loud the whole room shook. The door creaked behind me. I didn't have time to get up. I slashed

123

backwards with the letter opener and felt it connect. My dead-eyed double stood behind me, blood dripping from her shin, but she made no attempt to attack me. I bounced to my feet and took another swing at her, slashing a crimson ribbon across her chest.

And cried out in pain.

'Stupid brat,' hissed the girl who wasn't me. 'Think you can hurt me without hurting yourself?'

I looked down and saw identical crimson slashes across my chest and shin. I sucked in a breath. How the heck was I supposed to fight her? The fairground music suddenly quietened to a distant background noise. I backed away from Creepy Doppelganger Girl, looking round the room, and noticed I was reflected in every mirror. Oh no. That couldn't be good.

Even creepier, every mirror reflection had its back turned to me.

*Join in the contest, Tommy. It'll be an easy way to fit in, Tommy.* Who was the dorkface now?

Yet they didn't seem to be coming out from behind the glass. Instead they started to talk.

'Think you'll ever fit in here? What a joke!' said one behind me.

'You honestly think Jinx likes you? He just feels

124

sorry for you,' snarled another.

'Look at you, twelve years old and already damned to Hell. Evil child,' spat a mirror across from me.

They spoke in my voice, but a tone I'd never used: one seething with hatred.

But I had a secret weapon – Sparky. And judging by the singe on my hoody, he was busy living up to his name, which meant they were lying.

I stuck my chin out. '*Please.* You really think I'm scared of myself? You're all just glass and nothingness.'

All at once every reflection spun round to face me, and their faces were hollow-eyed grinning skulls.

'OK, that's actually quite scary,' I admitted.

'No wonder your mother abandoned you, couldn't stand to be with you,' hissed a skull to my right.

Sparky stayed motionless. My lip wobbled. 'Don't you dare talk about my mum!'

Soon every single mirror was hurling abuse at me and I couldn't tell when Sparky was sparking and when he wasn't any more, and it wasn't just words: it was things that I had thought myself, things that, on a bad day, I might have believed to be true. So much for sticks and stones. A fight, I could've handled. But this was so much worse. I threw the useless letter opener to the ground and slammed my hands over my ears.

And nearly brained myself with the tins of paint hanging from my arm.

*The paint.*

I picked up the letter opener, prised open a can and hurled the contents at the nearest mirror, splattering out the reflection behind it. The voice behind the mirror fell silent. Yes! I ran to the next and did it again, and again. All the while, the girl who wasn't me stood unmoving in the

centre of the room, not saying a word, just looking at me with an expression of deep loathing.

Several minutes later I had covered every mirror with paint and the room was quiet once more. I spun round, looking for the way out. But there was only one door – the one leading back the way I'd come.

No. There had to be a way out, it wasn't fair! Maybe that was what Lilith was up to. Maybe she was trying to trap me here forever. Or at least rip my self-esteem into confetti.

I sank to the floor, sniffing away tears. What now?

There was a movement in the corner of my eye. I spun round. There was one mirror I'd missed. But it wasn't reflecting the room I was in, or me – it showed the room back at Sharp Point. I let out a huge sigh of relief and ran over.

Just as I was about to walk through, the girl behind me laughed.

I turned round. 'I'll give you points for creepy,' I said. 'But I won. It's over.'

She tilted her head to one side and looked at me with her dead eyes. 'You are a nobody,' she said, almost apologetically. 'Without the D'Evils, what do you have? No family, no home, *nothing*. When she returns, Persephone will throw you out of the palace like a stray dog and you will be alone again. Abandoned. Unwanted. A miserable, pathetic, nobody.'

'I made it through this on my own!' I said, cheeks hot with rage and misery.

'And yet...you are still nothing without them, aren't you? You know it, too.' She shook her head sadly and vanished.

My stomach clenched in despair. She was right. I knew she was right.

I turned away and limped back through the mirror to safety.

*As schoolchildren wailed and bled about him, Percival gazed absent-mindedly out of the arched windows of the training hall and thought how pretty the swirling green skies of Hell were. Odd that he'd never noticed before. He hadn't felt this chipper since he'd persuaded that English commander to burn Joan of Arc at the stake.*

*Not that he'd actually plucked up courage to do anything so outlandish as to speak to Dragon Girl yet. But he'd spied her in the yard, talking gently to the dragons and petting them behind the ears, and he'd found out a little bit about her by asking around. Apparently she was one of the best dragon pilots in Pandemonium, and only 342 years old, which explained her dewy green skin and general air of chirpiness. Most importantly, she was single, and her name was Alethea. He still called her Dragon Girl in his head, though. It had a poetic ring to it.*

*He was also cheerier because there was nothing like watching a bunch of spoilt demon kids being chased by zeegles or their own worst nightmares to put a spring in your step. If he wasn't going to be deputy,* he could at least enjoy the carnage that came with the interview process.

The exit door flew open and another red-skinned, black-horned child fell into the room. This one was too stunned to speak. Percival made a note on his clipboard. All the candidates had entered the training room now, and nineteen were still to escape. Maybe by the time they reached the final trial there would be no one left, he thought hopefully. Then Lilith would have to give him the job.

Her Majestic Fiendishness had been even spikier than usual since finding out her son Dantalion had tried to take over from Lucifer and been locked up in Purgatory for his pains. Percival wasn't quite sure why, since Lilith never seemed to take much interest in her children, and he was pretty sure she didn't want Lucifer dethroned. But he supposed she took it as a personal affront to her power.

Another child fell out of the exit door. Percival sighed, made another note on his clipboard, then went back to looking out the window. The sky was the deep green of seaweed, and the mist swirled like it was trying to encircle the city and drag it down to the bottom of the ocean. Suddenly the room darkened. Two sets of scaly orange wings swooped down and skidded to a halt right beside the building. Percival couldn't believe it. Dragon Girl! He pictured himself shoving his clipboard at his gormless assistant and dashing outside to tell her how beautiful she was and how impressed he was with her dragonry skills. But he couldn't bring himself to do it. What if she laughed at him? Ignored him? Told him she didn't date fiends? She was so out of his league.

Alethea loosened the dragons' harnesses and settled into the driver's seat, a paperback in hand. Then she looked straight through the window and caught Percival staring at her.

Oh no.

He gave her a quick smile and a little wave and immediately wanted to thunk his head against the wall he was so mortified. But Dragon Girl didn't seem to mind. She gave him a broad grin in return.

And with that, Percival fell in love.

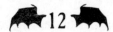

# All Creatures Great and Small

## JINX

I DASHED INTO the courtyard at Sharp Point, the academy's blood-red walls and pointed turrets looming overhead like a splayed ribcage. A group of freakishly neat cadets strode by and smirked nastily as I puffed past, brushing the messy hair out of my eyes. Boy, was I glad I'd got out of going to school here. I would've been the world's worst soldier. I couldn't even manage a trip to the library without causing carnage. I cursed myself again for losing the book. I'd never find it now – it'd be under a pile of rubble and a two-ton iron staircase. Oh well, I'd just have to try to remember what it had said.

Ahead, two double doors lay open and the crowd inside chattered excitedly. I burrowed my way to the front. I still didn't even know what this trial was. Were they watching the contestants fight hand to hand, like we'd thought?

Lilith had her head bent talking to the fiend with the comb-over. Aha! Maybe I could sleuth a bit. I crept closer, keeping the front line of the crowd in front of me, and craned to listen. And distinctly heard her hiss the word *Dantalion.*

I was so surprised, I tripped on my shoelace, fell past the person in front and landed at her feet. *Ow.* I was really not cut out to be a detective. Lilith clammed up immediately and glared down at me, yellow eyes thinned to slits.

'Sorry!' I picked myself up and hurried away. *Dantalion.* That was it. That was all I needed to know. Lilith must be planning a coup, just like her son had. Maybe she'd even been directing Dantalion's rebellion from Earth. Perhaps she'd been the criminal mastermind behind the whole thing.

I spotted Dad waving me over. And had an awful thought. The book hadn't said who had opened Pandora's Box. No one knew. But who would have wanted to let all the evils of the world loose on humanity? Who more than the Devil himself? Maybe these days Dad was more interested in playing golf and sending presents, but back in the old days... I took a deep breath. No. I didn't have any proof it had been Dad. In fact, the book hadn't even hinted at it. It couldn't have been him.

I put Pandora and Dantalion out of my mind and went over to him. 'What's the trial?' I asked.

He explained about some magic room of sins, and that Tommy had chosen vanity. He shook his head. 'I'm worried about her. She's been in there a long time.'

I shuffled my feet, wondering whether to tell him my suspicions about Lilith and Dantalion, or even ask him about Pandora.

'Are you all right?' he said.

'I'm fine.'

'OK.' He frowned at the exit door, clearly worried about Tommy. It wasn't a good time for questions and conspiracy theories. Come to think of it, if the King of Hell was worrying about Tommy, so should I. I forgot all about rebellions and magic boxes and demolished libraries and joined Dad in staring at the door, willing Tommy to come out.

And stared, and stared.

Three more kids came out. One was screaming, the other was dripping wet and half-drowned, and the third was pale as death and muttering to herself.

Dammit. I'd been so caught up in Tommy's Pandora mystery I'd forgotten Dad had warned us the contest would be dangerous. And now my best friend was stuck in some nightmare scenario dreamed up by Lilith.

A blonde girl staggered out, covered in white paint and bleeding from the chest – a blonde girl with freckles and brown eyes.

'Tommy!' I ran over to her.

'Jinx! You came!' She gave me a wan smile.

'Course I did, you nimrod. You're my best friend. Are you all right? You're bleeding.'

She looked down at her chest. 'I'll be OK. Hey, Your Royal Wickedness.'

Lucifer patted her on the shoulder. 'Well done, well done. Was getting a bit worried there for a minute.'

Tommy's wan smile turned into a beam and she waved her hand dismissively. 'Piece of cake. All smoke and mirrors. Although speaking of cake, I could really do with a slice of demon meringue pie. Or two.'

Dad smiled. 'Of course. I can give you kids a lift back to the palace. Don't you need to give your name to Percival?'

'Percival? Oh, you mean the head fiend? Right. Hang on a sec.' Tommy went over to the fiend with the comb-over, who was gazing out of the window.

'Tomasina Covelli,' she said.

His head snapped round and he took a startled step backwards.

Tommy sighed. 'Yes, news flash, I'm a Bonehead.

But I was invited.'

Percival looked like he'd swallowed his tongue. Finally he reached onto a table behind him and handed her a gold envelope. 'Details of the next trial,' he mumbled, staring at her.

Great, another demon who obviously hated Boneheads. I glared at him helpfully for her as we left the hubbub behind and followed Dad outside and round to the side of the building.

'Whoa.' Tommy took a step backwards.

'My rickshaw,' said Dad.

'That's a rickshaw like Darkangel Palace is a cosy little cottage,' said Tommy.

Two dragons with mottled orange and red scales pawed the ground before a gleaming black and gold open carriage.

Tommy nudged me. 'Why do you use actual rickshaws when you have *that*?'

'I'm not allowed to use it till I'm sixteen. Dad's worried I'll crash it. The dragons are pretty speedy.'

'You really are Good,' she said. 'I would so take it for a joyride.'

We bundled inside, Tommy and me facing Dad. The carriage lurched forward and in seconds we were whooshing through the air.

'This is so cool!' she said. 'Also, I didn't know dragons were actually a thing.'

Dad nodded. 'They're the original Hellish creatures. Centuries ago, some of them escaped to Earth and caused a bit of a kerfuffle. Took a lot of work to round them all up and bring them home again, I can tell you.'

'I'm not sure *dragons* and bit of a *kerfuffle* belong in the same sentence,' I said, looking out at the huge muscular beasts pulling the carriage.

Dad laughed.

'But wouldn't you *want* them on Earth?' asked Tommy. 'Causing kerfuffles?'

'Normally, absolutely. Unfortunately human weaponry improved and the dragons started losing, so we had to save them. They're happier here anyway, surrounded by fire and brimstone. It's their natural habitat.'

I poked Tommy in the side. 'So, what's in the magic envelope?'

'Huh? Oh, right.' She pulled the envelope out of her pocket and opened it. 'The third trial: answer this riddle. *How do you get blood out of a stone?*' She blew her cheeks out. 'No clue. Your Evilness?'

Dad shook his head. 'Oh no, this is for you to solve. I'm not getting involved. Lilith would have my guts for garters!'

I frowned. I didn't like Dad and Lilith being so chummy. It gave me a lurchy feeling in my belly. 'When's Mum home?' I said pointedly.

Dad broke into a grin. 'Fienday! Can't wait to see her.'

Tommy went back to peeling bits of paint off her jeans, and I looked at Dad, happily smiling to himself as he thought of Mum. It was hard to believe he'd open Pandora's Box. But if not him, then who had done it?

Then I had an idea. There was one other person in Hell who knew about Tommy's family, who might know if she was really descended from Pandora, or if the curse was real.

'Dad, you know Tommy's Uncle Boozy?' I asked.

Tommy's head shot up.

'That sweaty little man who sold his soul to me? Of course, what about him?'

'Do you have records? I mean, do you know exactly where he is in Hell?'

Tommy went pale. 'I'm not sure I want to know.'

'Scared you might bump into him?' said Dad. 'Well, don't worry. Unless I make an exception, like with Monsieur Rodin, all Sold Souls go to the same place – the brimstone factory. They're chained up and spend eternity mining or processing brimstone. So you'll never have to see him again.'

'The brimstone factory?' I said. 'Right here in Pandemonium?'

Any remaining colour drained from Tommy's face.

'Yes. Why?'

'Doesn't matter. Thanks.'

Tommy gave me a look but I turned to gaze down on the soaring spires of Pandemonium. Somewhere down there, there was someone who could give us answers. Granted, someone Tommy probably never wanted to see again in her life – or afterlife. But if she was cursed, we needed to find out more. We needed to uncurse her. And she was a tiny ninja girl. She could handle it.

We landed smoothly in the palace forecourt and said our goodbyes to Dad, who muttered something about going to check on a new monster he was developing.

'What was all that about?' asked Tommy as we jogged up the main staircase. She stopped for a breather when we reached the top and I remembered she'd hurt herself.

'You all right? Do you need to go to the doctor?'

'Nah, it's OK. Just a scratch.'

'You don't have to be all brave with me, you know. Even tiny ninjas need the odd Elastoplast.'

'Shut up.' But she cracked a smile as she carried on up the stairs to our floor. 'Just tell me what you were going on about in the carriage. Why do you care about Boozy?'

'I went to the library and found out some stuff about Pandora, and...look, why don't you go and get into some clothes that aren't dripping blood and paint, then I'll tell you all about it.'

We came to the landing outside my room. 'OK,' she said, looking too tired to argue further. She turned to walk down the covered bridge to her bedroom...shrieked, jumped back and landed on my foot. My toes crunched and I hopped up and down, shrieking alongside her.

The entire covered bridge was swarming with silvery

spikemoths – not just three or four, like in the rafters of my room, which wasn't a big deal. No, hundreds of them, so many that the buzzing was like an angry lawnmower. Which was a very big deal. Then they noticed us. The buzzing grew even louder, and the spikemoths swirled into a spiral formation like a thousand tiny arrowheads…which shot right at us.

'Aaaargh!'

I grabbed Tommy's shoulder and yanked her backwards. We fell into my room and I slammed the door behind us. Several spikemoths had landed on her and she flailed around, trying to throw them off. I grabbed a book and squished them as they fell to the floor. Tommy yanked off her hoody and spun round and round.

'Are they gone? Are they gone?'

'Yes, that's it, they're all gone.'

But then her lip wobbled. She lifted her T-shirt and squealed. A moth was strolling nonchalantly across her belly button. Before I could do anything, Sparky slid out of her jeans pocket and ate the moth in one bite.

After several more minutes' flapping, I finally managed to calm her down.

'They're really all gone this time. Really,' I said.

'I. Hate. Hellbeasts,' she growled. She stroked Sparky. 'But *you* are a lifesaver.' Sparky belched happily. 'Please tell me what on Earth all that was about.'

I was as flummoxed as her. 'No idea. Never seen as many of them as that, or swarming like that. And I know I tell you not to worry about them, but still...they *can* sting. Hundreds of them like that...it's dangerous.'

That was the point where she lost it, just a tiny bit. 'Someone's trying to kill me!' she wailed.

My mouth went dry. 'What?'

Tommy ranted about the graffiti and dreadbeasts and being the only human in a city full of demons and how everyone hated her. 'And now this! Don't tell me it's a coincidence.'

'OK, OK, I believe you.' I stuck my eye to the keyhole. 'You know you can't actually die, though, right? You're already dead. Deceased. Finished.'

'Shut up. I still have no desire to get stung to bits. Are they still there?'

I nodded grimly. 'I'll sort this out.' I picked up the phone and arranged for some serfs to come and get rid of the moths. Within minutes the corridor outside was busy with flapping and squawking Boneheads.

Tommy sat on the window ledge and blew her fringe out of her eyes. 'Since we're stuck here, you want to tell me what you found out about Pandora? And why you were asking questions about Boozy?'

I flopped into the desk chair and spun round. 'Right. Well... bit of a problem. (a) It looks like Pandora wasn't actually an evil queen – in fact she probably wasn't evil at all. And (b) you kind of might have a little problem with being cursed for all eternity.'

'What?'

'Um, curse. There's a curse. Sorry about that. But, uh, you've already ended up in Hell so probably that's finished now.' I thought about the spikemoths and graffiti. *Or not.*

Tommy hugged her knees. 'Oh, this just gets better and better. Is there any good news?'

'Yeah...no.'

'Is there more bad news?'

'Yes.'

She looked up at the ceiling as though it had personally offended her. 'Let me have it.'

'Well, your uncle, you see. If you are cursed – and all those old books are always full of curses and warnings and prophecies so it's probably a load of hogwash – but, if you are, then your uncle might know something about it. He's your mum's brother, isn't he?'

'Yeah.'

'So maybe he knows whether you're really descended from Pandora, or something about the curse.'

Tommy grimaced. 'You think we should go and talk to him?'

'Not if you don't want. It's just an idea.'

'You really think I'm cursed?'

'No. I don't know. But I think we should try to find out. Then if you are, we can try to figure out a way to break the curse, and if you're not...you don't have to worry about it any more.'

She narrowed her eyes. 'I wasn't worrying about it at all five minutes ago.'

'Sorry. But I thought you'd want to know.'

Tommy sighed. 'Yeah, you're right. Just not every day you get chased by your evil mirror twin, attacked by spikemoths, *and* find out you're cursed for eternity. Bit of a rubbish afternoon.'

I sat up. 'Evil mirror twin?'

She shook her head. 'Long story.'

I frowned at her glum face and remembered what she'd said about wanting to fit in. At this rate she really was going to want to run off to the Himalayas with Lilith. I needed to do something to cheer her up. Then I had an idea. I peeked through the keyhole.

'Come on, the coast's clear, let's go and see Dad.'

'Your dad? Why? Are you going to tell him about Pandora?'

'Um, no. I don't exactly have any proof anyway. Had a bit of a mishap in the library.'

Tommy smirked. 'Bottomless abysses again?'

'Not quite that bad. Come on, I'll tell you about it on the way.'

The one thing I hadn't told Tommy was that I thought there was a chance Dad might be mixed up in the Pandora story. I decided to keep that to myself for now. It was probably nothing anyway.

'You know, it's possible those weren't meant for you,' I said as we trudged through the palace. 'The spikemoths. I wouldn't put it past my nemeses Benny and Arael. They're always winding me up. Maybe they miss bullying me at school.'

'Oh, I think I met them. Red-skinned, one kind of looks like a baby weasel, the other has a face like a squashed warthog?'

I smirked. 'That's them.'

'Gave weasel boy a good kick in the shin.'

'I knew I liked you.'

'Guess we're the two most popular people in Hell, huh? No wonder we ended up mates.'

I grabbed her shoulder. 'Oh, I nearly forgot! Lilith is totally planning a coup!'

She gave me a stern look. 'Not this again.'

'No, seriously this time. I heard her mention Dantalion.'

She raised an eyebrow. 'Really? But...he is her son. Doesn't necessarily mean anything. Did you hear anything else?'

'No,' I admitted. I didn't admit that was because I'd been too busy falling over my own feet.

When we got to Dad's study we found the Prince of Lies with his feet up on the desk reading a magazine called *The Modern Demon*. '101 Ways To Be More Vindictive!' boasted the cover.

I waved my arms about dramatically as I told him about the graffiti and rampaging dreadbeasts and the attack of the killer spikemoths.

Dad put his elbows on his desk and rubbed his forehead. 'Oh dear. Tommy, I'd hoped I wouldn't have to tell you about this, but there have been...dissidents.'

She squinted at him. 'Dissi-whats?'

'Some demons who weren't too happy about my taking in a human girl. I've got three of them in the dungeons right now. I'll go and have a little chat with them and see if they've got any accomplices. I'm so sorry about all this. I feel like a terrible host.' He looked genuinely embarrassed. 'I'm going to post guards at the bottom of the stairs going up to both your bedrooms, and if you go into town, I want you to use my chariot, OK?'

Tommy's face lit up.

I did a discreet fist-pump. I'd hoped Dad would suggest that. I knew it would cheer her up.

'You will, of course, have a driver,' added Dad.

Dammit.

'Thanks, Your Badness,' said Tommy. 'Dragons make everything better.'

Dad smiled. 'Now that sounds like a pretty good motto.'

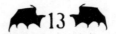 

# Fire and Brimstone and Other Non-fluffy Things

TOMMY

MY *DEAD GIRL'S Guide to Hell* had a brand new chapter now – one that wasn't just about Hellish flora and fauna, or demon etiquette. I read the page one last time.

- The Bad News: I might be cursed for eternity. Which could explain getting squished by a lion, being sent to Hell, and almost dying all over again a hundred different times, not to mention the nasty graffiti and killer spikemoth attacks.

- The Badder News: I have to go and talk to Boozy about it.

- The Even Badder News: It's Worseday today. Which means Persephone comes home the day after tomorrow.

- The Only Vague Ray of Good News: I'm still in the contest. Maybe that'll impress the Terror of the Boneheads enough so she doesn't throw me out. That's if a hellbeast doesn't eat me first.

'Ready?' asked Jinx, poking his horned head round my bedroom door.

I stuck the page in a drawer, threw the last of my Spikemoth Attack clothes down the laundry chute with a shudder and pulled on a clean hoody. 'As I'll ever be. Not *massively* looking forward to seeing Boozy again. Don't think he's going to be very happy to see me. On the bright side, I think Sparky might make quite a good bodyguard.' I pointed at the little shocktopus who was furiously trying to set fire to the desk.

'Also, dragons,' said Jinx.

'Also dragons.' I grinned.

I slid Sparky into a pocket and said goodbye to Grrr and Argg, who were having a thumb war outside the window. 'Keep an eye on my room, would you?'

'☀☻ ⚡←☺▣☊♣♯,' said Arrg, pulling his teeth back into a skull-ish smile.

'Thanks.'

'Not bringing Bruce?' I asked Jinx as we jogged

down the stairs.

'Nah. I don't want him to fly off and get lost in the mines. We might never find him again.'

'What if *we* get lost in the mines?'

'We'll probably die horribly.'

'OK, just checking.'

We left the palace and walked through the soft autumn air round to the stables at the side. A slim, green demon with tall, twisting horns was feeding one of the dragons out of a sack – a bulging, wriggling sack.

'Um, excuse me,' I said, trying not to look inside.

The green demon bowed. 'I've been expecting you. My name is Alethea and I'll be your driver for today. Please, climb aboard.' She hopped up into the front and Jinx and I climbed up after her.

I glanced back at the palace and froze as I noticed one of the creepy fiends watching us from a window – the one with the comb-over. Ugh. Except it wasn't us he was watching – it was our new driver. And he was watching her with a dreamy expression on his face, like he had a crush. I smirked. Just when I thought Hell couldn't get any weirder.

Before I could point him out to Jinx, Alethea shook the reins. 'Where to, young prince?' she asked again.

I rolled my eyes. In his jeans, black jumper, and scuffed

trainers, Jinx hardly looked like royalty.

'Brimaeus's brimstone factory please.'

'Yes, sir.'

The driver whispered something to her dragons and we lurched off into the air.

I leant out of the open carriage and gazed over the bustling streets, demons scuttling far below.

'You sure you're OK with this?' asked Jinx. 'Talking to your uncle?'

'Not really. Seeing how the last time I saw him I

151

accidentally fed him to a lion.'

Jinx snorted.

'So I don't think he's going to be very happy to see me. But he's also pretty stupid, especially with the whole selling his soul to the Devil thing, so I'm not *that* worried. And if I really am cursed, I want to know about it.'

The wind blew into my face, making my eyes water, and I smelled the factory before I saw it. It was out on the eastern outskirts, as far from the centre as possible, I guessed to keep the horrible stench out of the nicer parts of the city. Slim white chimneys towered up into the sky like cigarettes, yellow smoke coughing from them.

'I'll wait here for you, sir, madam,' said Alethea as we landed.

We hopped down, and she pulled out a gaudy pink paperback and settled down to read something called *Demon's Delight*.

Jinx and I looked up at the entrance to Brimaeus's. The carved stone archway showed a relief of souls in torment.

'Nice artwork,' I said. 'Come on, let's get this over with.'

'I hope your uncle works in administration,' said Jinx. 'I don't fancy having to wander round the lower reaches of the mine.'

We went under the gates and I started. 'Did that just

move?' I pointed up at the archway. Yup. The souls in torment were definitely wriggling.

Jinx shrugged.

I hurried on by, shuddering. 'Never mind, I should know by now that everything here moves. Ugh.'

'You're just jealous 'cos carvings on Earth are boring and never move a muscle. Anyway, you like the gargoyles.'

'I guess.' They were smiley, though, not writhing in agony.

We crossed the forecourt, past three red lorries with *Brimaeus's: Best for Brimstone, Worst for Boneheads!* emblazoned on the side. Nice.

Before us loomed a big sliding warehouse door, open to the factory. Hammering and yelling and the worst stench I'd ever smelled wafted from inside. Rows of manacled humans hefted pallets of brimstone, shining bright yellow and crystalline, from a conveyor belt into various machines. I stared at them. So this was where Boozy was.

To the right of the warehouse was a glassed-in office. Jinx knocked on the door and we went in. Two besuited red-skinned demons sat at desks typing furiously. On one wall was a sign with a grinning demon saying: *You don't have to be evil to work here, but it helps!* Behind them, a demon with the head of a cougar sat at a desk piled high with files, shouting into a telephone.

'I don't care if he lost an arm!' she growled. 'Sew it back on again! That's no excuse for missing a day of work.' She looked up at me and Jinx and her eyes thinned to slits. She yelled into the phone a bit more then slammed down the receiver. 'Yes?'

I was glad I was feeling a bit more confident after flying here in a chariot literally pulled by dragons. All the same, I stepped back to let royalty boy work his magic.

'Jinx D'Evil,' he said. 'My father's asked me to speak to one of the...er...inmates here.'

'Fine, fine. Name?'

'Jinx...'

'Not your name, you cretin, the Bonehead's name.'

Jinx went even redder than usual.

'Reginald Bosworthy,' I said.

'One moment.' She tapped at her computer a few times. 'Bosworthy. Arrived this year, yes? He's down in Grimmest Mine.'

'Grimmest Mine?'

Cougar woman rolled her eyes. 'There are five levels. Factory floor, where we are now, below us Research and Development, and then far below are the three mines: Grim, Grimmer, Grimmest. Your Bonehead

154

is deep underground.'

Phooey. Why was nothing ever easy?

The manager looked at me with hooded eyes. 'You're taking your serf with you?' she asked Jinx.

Serfs were the damned humans who worked as servants in Pandemonium. I crossed my arms, furious. 'I am no—'

Jinx flapped his hands. 'This is Tommy, who is a guest of my father's. She is *not* a serf, and yes she is accompanying me.'

The manager continued to stare at me. A whisper of a smile played at the corner of her mouth. 'Your funeral,' she said with a shrug. She scrabbled around on her desk for a minute and produced a keycard. 'Come with me.'

We followed her back out of the office and onto the factory floor. My bones shook with the rattle of machinery and shouts of the workers. I wondered what they'd each sold their souls for, and whether it had been worth it.

The cougar demon pointed one golden paw to a metal door at the side. 'Use this keycard to operate the lift. Once you get down to the mine level, you'll have to use the local transport to take you all the way down to Grimmest Mine.'

'Local transport?' I didn't like the sound of that. Knowing Hell we'd have to ride on the back of an ogre or something.

But the manager had already turned and stalked off back towards her office.

Jinx side-eyed me, looking twitchy.

'What did she mean by "your funeral"?' I said.

Jinx stuck the keycard in the lift and the metal doors shooshed open. 'That there'll be singing? And also snacks. I expect.' He stepped into the lift.

'Right.'

'Maybe a tiny bit of death.'

'Oh goody.' I took a deep breath and got in after him. The doors slammed shut. 'Here goes nothing.'

The lift dropped so fast my stomach shot up by my ears. We both grabbed at the railing and hung on tight. Just as I was convinced we were plunging to our deaths, it screeched to a stop and the doors burst open, letting in a billowing cloud of stinking yellow smoke. I covered my mouth and gagged.

'Eww. Smells like someone ate too many baked beans.'

'That's brimstone for you.' Jinx pulled his hoody up over his nose and stepped out, and I followed suit. We were in a forked corridor blasted out of the rock. A dusty sign pointed straight ahead to Grim Mine, with another arrow pointing right to Grimmer Mine. In the distance, muffled hammering and crunching noises and the occasional yelp echoed out. Jinx took the right-hand corridor and I followed reluctantly, stroking Sparky in the pouch of my hoody. He may've only been the size of a large gobstopper, but he made me feel safer.

The hammering noises grew louder and louder, and as we came out of the corridor I gasped, then broke into a coughing fit. We were on a rocky platform overlooking a vast, cylindrical, yellow cavern that had been carved into the brimstone. It rose fifty feet into the air above, and plunged down so deep I couldn't see the bottom. Hanging from the rock walls were hundreds of humans on tiny wooden platforms, hacking away with pickaxes and filling buckets with brimstone, which they then attached to wires that crisscrossed the mine. It looked like the inside of a beehive. The buckets zoomed off this way and that, but the air was so hazy with brimstone mist it was hard to see where to.

I finally stopped coughing and looked at Jinx. He wiped his eyes, which were nearly as red as his skin.

'The brimstone is just annoying to me, but it can be toxic to humans. Try not to breathe any in.'

Great. I pulled a face, but kept my mouth shut.

Jinx pointed over my shoulder to a sign on the wall.

## IT HAS BEEN _0_ DAYS SINCE OUR LAST ACCIDENT.

The zero had what looked like dried blood on it. Lovely.
I walked past it to where a small metal cart stood waiting
on one end of the rocky platform. A thin set of tracks

snaked away from it down into the mine. Oh boy. So this was the local transport. Well, that didn't look death-defying at all. There was a brake, and two pairs of wooden seats with straps. On the back was a rickety-looking engine, presumably for coming back up again. And that was all. No roof. No steering wheel. Brilliant.

Something flickered in the corner of my vision. I turned to see a flame float across the vast yellow cavern. Then I spotted another, and another. I squinted harder. Flames *with eyes*. I squeaked.

Jinx saw them too. I pulled a quizzical face.

He shrugged. 'Don't know what they—'

One of the flame creatures wafted across and floated beneath a miner. The miner shrieked, and started hacking harder at the rock face.

Ah, fiery fascist overseers. Well, that was nice.

'Maybe let's not hang around,' said Jinx.

I jumped into the cart and strapped myself in. Jinx did the same, nodded grimly at me then yanked the brake. For a second nothing happened. The cart tipped forward, forward...then we were thrown back in our seats as we screeched round and round the circular sides of the mine like we were on the world's most dangerous rollercoaster – which we basically were. It was half terrifying, half

159

exhilarating. I might've screamed a bit.

Tears flew from my eyes as we sped faster and faster, past the hammering humans and flying buckets of brimstone and flame monsters and into the yellow smoke. Just in time, the fug cleared and I saw a platform looming below us. I threw myself forward and heaved on the brake. It squealed like a terrified warthog and we clattered to a halt, panting.

OK, we'd made it. I staggered out on wobbly legs and clutched the wall – where a sign hung, proclaiming 'Grimmer Mine'. Oh, badgers. We weren't there yet. We had to go deeper.

Jinx was already trotting across the platform to the next cart. I sighed and followed him. It was hotter down here. Beads of sweat trickled down my back. Stupid Boozy. He'd better have some answers after all this. We strapped ourselves in, shared an unhappy glance, then set off once more. We plunged deeper and deeper, the cart bumping and rattling along the spiralling rails. The air grew hotter and hotter, so thick that I could taste it, so thick that it felt like I was burning.

I looked at my sleeve. I *was* burning.

'Tommy!' yelled Jinx. 'You're on fire!'

A cluster of flame monsters had attached themselves

to the cart. I flapped my arm desperately and sent one shooting off into space.

'Bonehead,' said one, in a rustling voice.

The others took up the chant. 'Bonehead, Bonehead, Bonehead. Get back to work, Bonehead.'

I smelled my hair singeing. The cart hurtled on, bouncing off walls, as I smacked at my smoking clothes. *Your funeral.* The evil old bag. She'd known a Bonehead wouldn't be safe down here.

Jinx ripped off his jacket and slapped it at the creatures, but they ducked and dived and came back, trying to set me on fire. I yanked a throwing star out of my pocket but it grew so hot I was forced to drop it. Sweat poured down my face and everything stank of burnt hair and blackened clothes and we were both going to die and it wasn't going to matter if I was cursed or not because I'd be doubly dead and ahhhhh—

The platform appeared in front of my nose and Jinx yanked on the brake but it was too late. The cart slammed into the rock, let out an almighty crack and tipped forward, tearing off our seatbelts and sending us both flying through the air. For about three seconds, my afterlife flashed before my eyes – and not even the good bits, the bit where I was being chased by a carnivorous carousel horse (thanks a lot, brain) – then I hit rock hard and landed in a heap.

Jinx swore loudly behind me. I jumped to my feet, my elbow throbbing, whirling around after the fire things. But they had vanished. I looked round and saw why. This platform was surrounded by glass, and we had burst straight through two plexiglass doors that had slammed shut behind us. The mine cart lay upended several feet from the tracks, and the fire monsters clustered against the pane, flashing eyes furious, wild animals deprived of their prey.

Jinx picked himself up off the ground. 'You all right?' he said.

I rubbed my bloodshot eyes and glared at him. 'Apart from a strong urge to strangle you. What were those things?'

'Never seen them before. Guess they're here to make sure the Sold Souls work hard. They must've confused you with the other Boneheads. Sorry?'

I growled.

He winced. 'Please don't spike me in my sleep.'

'That's not a bad idea.'

'Come on, this'll all be worth it when we get rid of your curse. Maybe things will stop trying to toast you then.'

'Nothing would've been trying to toast me if I'd been home playing Mario Kart.' I sighed and checked on Sparky who threw an irritated spark or three into the air. 'Sorry about that, bud.'

I brushed all the foul-smelling brimstone ash from my clothes and looked around. 'There,' I said, pointing to a thick steel door at the back of the platform.

We stumbled over, pulled it open and went through. The door whooshed shut behind us, closing with a loud click.

I spun round, panicked. 'Is that a magic door? Are we locked in here forever?'

'Um, no. Hydraulics.'

'Oh.'

'Come on.'

We set off down another rocky corridor. At the end, behind a door with a glass panel in it, was another glassed-in platform, but this one looked like a control room. A long dashboard filled with computer screens and multicoloured switches curved round the front. One red-skinned demon sat with his back to us. I pushed the door open and went in.

The demon spun round, the bags under his eyes wobbling with surprise. 'Who are you?'

I nudged Jinx.

He squared his skinny shoulders. 'Jinx D'Evil. We need to talk to a Bonehead down here. Reginald...'

'Bosworthy,' I finished.

The demon ran a fat hand across his face. 'Nobody tells me anything,' he muttered. 'One moment.' He turned back to his control console and typed away at a screen. Then he flicked a switch and leant down to speak into a microphone. 'Gallimeus, please bring Sold Soul 8301 to the manager's office immediately, Sold Soul 8301. Thank you.'

I breathed a sigh of relief. We wouldn't have to brave any more fire monsters to look for him. Plus it wasn't like Boozy could do anything with other people around. Like trying to kill me.

'Have a seat,' said the manager.

We slumped into spinning chairs along the console.

'But don't touch anything, please,' he added.

We spun our chairs away from the dashboard of flickering lights and screens and looked at each other.

'Well,' I said, 'we made it.' Which meant that any minute now I was going to see my uncle again. I felt sick at the thought. I changed the subject. 'So, any idea what Snake Queen's up to yet?'

Jinx sighed. 'Not really. I mean, she mentioned

Dantalion, so I'm super-suspicious, but I haven't found out anything new.'

I remembered Lilith's hand on Lucifer's arm. But it might not have been anything. She and Lucifer had been married once, after all. They could still be friendly.

'What?' said Jinx.

I shook my head. 'Nothing.'

'Tommy...'

'What about the spikemoth attack? Has your dad found out who—'

The room shook and a square in the floor in front of us slid open with a puff of orange smoke. Two figures rose out of the opening. I scrambled backwards in my chair. 'What the...'

The manager stood up. 'Thank you, Gallimeus. Master D'Evil, here is Sold Soul 8301. You may begin questioning him.'

Before us stood a stocky blue-skinned demon in denim overalls, holding the chains which bound his prisoner. A horribly familiar prisoner – a fat, sweaty man with more hair growing out of his ears and nose than from his head, and small, close-set eyes that made him look perpetually suspicious.

*Boozy.* I gripped the edge of my seat so tightly my

knuckles turned white. All the words I'd planned to say fell out of my head.

Jinx coughed and stood up. 'Thank you.' The hole in the floor clanged shut and the remnants of smoke faded away. Jinx glanced at me. 'Tommy...?'

I got slowly to my feet. 'Uncle Boozy. Nice to see you.' The words came out croakily, like an unoiled engine.

Boozy gaped at me, sweat dripping from his brow into his beady eyes. 'You!' he said, and lunged at me. Before I could yell out, Gallimeus had yanked him back by the chains attached to his wrists and ankles.

I took a deep breath and crossed my arms. Even if he scared me a bit, I refused to show it. 'You don't get to yell at me, it's your fault I'm here. I only want to ask you something. I'm not here to cause trouble.'

Boozy laughed – a desperate, cracking sound. 'Cause trouble? *Cause trouble?* You killed me, you weasel-faced brat!'

'Maybe a little bit,' I admitted. 'Anyway, I want to ask you something. Please. If you ever loved my mum at all, please help me.'

Boozy stopped pulling on his chains and narrowed his eyes. 'What's in it for me?'

'What?'

'I said, what's in it for me? If I help you, are you going to get me out of this hellhole?'

*Badgers.* I hadn't thought of that. Of course he'd want something in return.

Jinx turned to the manager. 'If he helps us, could you maybe—'

'No!' I said, suddenly furious. 'You haven't learnt a thing, have you, Boozy? You still blame everyone else for what happens to you. I can't believe you're my mum's brother. She was sweet and kind, she would never—'

Boozy cackled. 'Sweet and kind? She abandoned you,

you brat, or have you forgotten that? I was the one who looked after you. Me!'

Heat rushed through me, and tears pricked my eyes. 'She didn't mean to...she, she probably just lost track of us! She couldn't find me.'

Gallimeus sighed. 'This family reunion is delightful, but will you be much longer? I've got work to do, you know.'

'Just a minute more, please,' said Jinx.

Boozy's face twisted in spite. 'She knew exactly where you were. She didn't trust herself, that's all! My loony little sister. You know why she left you? *She heard voices.* Voices that told her *to kill you.*' He spat out the words, like a snake spitting venom. 'You were lucky she abandoned you. Otherwise she'd have murdered you.'

I fell back into my chair, my head spinning. 'No...'

'Yes.'

Gallimeus rolled his eyes.

Jinx stepped forward. 'Look, we just want to know about Tommy's family history. Does the name Pandora mean anything to you?'

'There was a barmaid I knew once,' said Boozy with a leer.

Jinx clenched his fists.

I sat shaking in my chair, trying not to cry. Because

Sparky was in my pocket. And he hadn't shocked me when my uncle had said those things. So they had to be true.

*My mum had wanted to kill me.*

Jinx tried again. 'Is there anything you can tell us? Anything at all? Maybe about a family curse?'

Boozy crossed his arms, clanking his chains and dragging Gallimeus sideways. 'Maybe I do, maybe I don't. Like I said, what's in it for me?'

I shook my head, feeling numb. 'He doesn't know anything. He's just playing with us.' I turned to the manager. 'Thank you for your help. We're finished here.'

Boozy's eyes widened in panic. 'No, wait! I'll help you, really, please, just get me out of here, I'll do anything!'

That was it. I stood up and snarled at him. 'No. You deserve everything you get. You're a nasty, spiteful, selfish little man, and—'

Boozy howled and threw himself at me. The bored Gallimeus was caught off guard and the chains slipped through his grasp. Jinx tried to jump between us but tripped over a chair. I scrambled backwards and smacked into the console, lighting up a row of red switches.

And the hole in the floor shot open, plunging a screaming Boozy out of the control room and into the depths of the mine.

We all rushed forward and peered down. Boozy had landed on the lift a floor below. He shook his fists and swore up at us, his face purple with rage.

*Good.*

I wiped my eyes then tugged Jinx's sleeve. 'Come on, let's go home.'

He nodded silently.

Jinx persuaded Gallimeus and the manager to lift the mine cart back onto the tracks and call off the flaming overseers. They hovered nearby, flickering angrily as we chugged slowly back up to Grimmer Mine and onto Grim, but didn't attack. All the time, I didn't say a word. In the lift, the smell of burning still filling my nostrils, I stared at the floor, feeling empty and sick.

'I totally get it now,' said Jinx.

I continued to stare at my feet. 'Get what?'

'Why you fed him to a lion. He's horrible.'

'Oh. I still didn't mean to, though. Not really. But I'm not sorry about it. Not any more. I thought meeting him would make me feel extra guilty, but after what he said...'

'Wait a minute. He said your mum heard voices, right? Telling her to kill you?'

I bit my lip hard. 'Thanks for reminding me.'

The lift clanged to the top and we got out. Jinx grabbed

my arm. 'But no, listen! Before Boozy was eaten, you got a sudden urge to pull the lion's ears, remember? I thought that sounded weird at the time. And now your mum...'

I yanked my arm free. 'Jinx, I really don't want to talk about it, OK?'

'But that's it, don't you see? You've got your answer! This *must* be to do with Pandora's curse. The curse was trying to make your mum do something terrible to ruin her life. But she loved you too much. So she sent you away to protect you.'

I stared at him. 'You...you really think so?'

'Yes! Think about it, it totally makes sense!'

I thought about it. And thought some more. My mum leaving was such a huge part of who I was. I was like a stick of rock with 'abandonment issues' stamped through it. But if she'd only done it to save me, if she hadn't been able to help it... My chest began to heave and my head spun. I wobbled and Jinx grabbed me by the shoulders.

'Whoa, easy there. Don't go all hyperventilate-y on me.'

I took a few deep breaths. *Mum left me at the circus to protect me.*

Jinx lifted my chin with a finger and looked into my eyes.

'Your mum never wanted to abandon you. She was trying to save you! And when the curse didn't work on your mum, it moved on to you instead. Hence you being the unluckiest human since ever.'

I finally got my breath back. Jinx was right, it all made sense. It seemed more unreal than any of the monsters in Hell, but it made sense. A smile pulled at my mouth. 'She didn't want to abandon me,' I repeated.

Jinx shook his head, grinning.

'She did love me, after all.'

'Of course she did.'

'It was all the curse!' we said in unison.

I broke into the world's widest grin and gave Jinx a bone-crushing hug. 'This is the best day of my life.'

'Afterlife.'

'I'll take it.'

# Us Girls

TOMMY SKIPPED ACROSS the factory floor, a huge grin on her face.

I jogged after her...stepped in a puddle and skidded across the room, landing in a heap by the exit doors. *Ow.* I looked down and saw I was covered in melted brimstone. Which was like being dipped in custard – really smelly custard. *Gross.* I scrambled to my feet, expecting to see Tommy laughing at me, but she stood frozen. Uh oh. What now?

'What was that riddle?' she said.

'What?'

'The riddle, for the next part of the contest?'

'You had to find a way to get blood out of a stone, I've still no idea—'

'Look, you wally!' She pointed at the puddle of brimstone, which was now dripping off my clothes and hands – the *red* puddle. Of *course.* When brimstone

173

melted it looked exactly like blood.

'Nice work!' I headed off towards Alethea and the carriage. 'Come on, let's go home. I'm starving.'

A little while later we were back in Salome Hall, handing over a yellow chunks of brimstone to Percival, along with about a dozen other kids. Tommy stared at the piece of paper the fiend had given her in return with the second riddle on it.

'What does it say? What's next in Lilith's Fun Festival of Doom?' I asked.

She gave me the note.

*I bring death from above and below. I am the original denizen of Hell. Steal my weapon.*

'I have absolutely no clue what that means,' said Tommy, 'but I am totally scared.'

I grinned. 'I know exactly what it is. This'll be easy.'

'Tell me then, brainbox.'

'I thought you were the one who was supposed to be doing this contest.'

She glared at me. 'I am also the one who has two throwing stars in her pocket.'

'OK, OK. The riddle means...we're going to see our

chauffeur again.'

We left the palace and went back out to the stables, where we found Alethea brushing one of the dragons with oil.

'Keeps her coat nice and supple,' she said.

Lacking even the tiniest bit of knowledge about dragon beauty treatments, I kept quiet. 'Could you do us a favour?' I asked. 'We need a dragon tooth. Would that be poss—'

'A dragon tooth!' said Tommy. 'The original hellbeast's weapon. Of course.'

Alethea wandered through to the back of the stables then came back carrying a tooth as long as my forearm. 'Bessie lost a milk tooth last night. Here you go.'

Tommy's eyes grew wide. 'That's a *baby* tooth?'

Alethea chuckled. 'Sure is.'

'Thank you.'

'Now death from above and below is sorted – food,' I said.

'Deal.'

'So,' I said, as we traipsed upstairs to the dining room, 'awesome news, your Uncle Boozy is getting exactly what he deserves. More awesome news: your mum didn't really want to abandon you.'

Tommy grinned from ear to ear. Then her smile slipped a bit. 'Less awesome, if she was hearing voices because of the Pandora curse, she might still be hearing them, wherever she is. So we still have to figure out a way to break the curse. What did your library book say about it?'

I sighed. 'Nothing. Just that Pandora and her bloodline were cursed for all eternity because she failed to make an unbreakable box.'

'Bit harsh. They could've just asked for a refund.'

'Oh, wait, it did say – this part was odd, so I remember it – it said the box was made from *the daggers of the earth*. And I remember the picture of the box. It was all woven, like a basket.'

Tommy pouted. 'Daggers of the earth, seriously? Why is

everything in old books always in riddles?'

'They didn't have TV back then? Had to make their own entertainment? Beats me. I know – since Babel was pretty useless, we could try the art workshop. I bet there's stuff there going back thousands of years.'

'And it's where we found the original portrait of Pandora.'

'Exactly. Maybe there are more paintings of her.'

As we neared the end of the hallway, I heard voices coming from the white and gold double doors at the end. I pressed one finger to my lips and we crept closer and stuck our ears to the wood. It was Dad and Lilith.

'I *have* missed this place,' said Lilith warmly.

'And I've missed you,' said Dad.

I scowled.

Lilith huffed. 'Can't have missed me that much. The minute I turned my back you went off and married that spring goddess. She's not even a demon, Luce!'

Dad growled, like this was a complaint he'd heard a hundred times. 'For evil's sake, Lilith, *we were on a break*! And *you* instantly went off and married that volcano demon, if I recall.'

'It was a phase. Lava reminded me of the fiery lake.'

'You always did prefer Earth to Hell,' grumbled Dad. 'Never understood why.'

'You had your kingdom. I wanted my own. The humans treated me like the queen I was.'

'Because they were terrified of you.'

'That was the fun part. Well, that and all the palaces and parties.'

Lucifer chuckled. 'And you always did like a good party. Can't imagine you get many of those now you're locked away in the Himalayas.'

Lilith sighed. 'Yes, life has been a bit quiet of late. Maybe it's time for a change of scene...'

There was silence.

Tommy frowned at the door.

Oh no. Maybe I'd got it all wrong. Maybe it wasn't plotting a coup Lilith was up to at all – maybe she wanted Dad back! I shoved the door open and burst into the dining room. Dad was leaning nonchalantly against the mantelpiece. Lilith sat at the table in a glittering green dress cut to the navel, sipping a glass of wine, a necklace shaped like a black snake twisting around her neck.

'Oh, um, hi,' I said. I gave an awkward little finger wave.

'Hello, kids,' said Dad. 'What have you been up to today?'

What had we been up to? Almost getting burnt to death, mostly. Maybe best not to mention that.

'Hello,' blurted Tommy, 'I'm so hungry I could eat a gavron.'

Dad laughed and pulled a bell cord hanging from the ceiling. Instantly the back doors opened and four serfs swooped in carrying gleaming silver platters.

Tommy and I sat down opposite Lilith, and Dad slipped into the chair at the head of the table.

'What happened to your hair?' Dad asked Tommy. There was a blackened clump in the middle of her shiny blonde parting, courtesy of the fiery factory overseers.

'Oh, my fault – stood too near the hairdryer. That old dragon still has a bit of spark in him.' She shrugged.

I breathed a sigh of relief.

'Sorry about that. I'll have a new one sent right up,' said Dad. 'So how are you doing at Lilith's latest puzzle quest?'

'I solved both riddles,' Tommy said smugly. I kicked her under the table. 'Er, with a little help from Jinx.' Then she looked worried. 'Um, that's OK, isn't it?'

Lilith beamed at her. 'But of course! You're doing so well. You're clearly very talented.'

Tommy dug at the tablecloth with her fork. 'Oh, um, thank you.'

There was silence for a few moments as we ate our kraken soufflés. When we'd finished, the serfs glided in and took our plates away, coming back seconds later with the next course of spiced dreadmeat casserole. I thought about the dreadbeasts chasing us across the Pale Pastures and ate mine vengefully.

Lilith pushed her plate to one side and leant forward. 'You know, I really think you'd like my fortress in the Himalayas, Tommy. Wouldn't you like to see the sky again? I mean the real sky, not this green Hellish one. It'd be nice to have a little girl around the place. All my children are grown now.' She actually managed to look vaguely kindly.

I narrowed my eyes at her. 'Aren't hidden mountain lairs a bit passé for supervillains?'

'Jinx!' Dad glared at me, but Lilith just laughed, although it didn't reach her eyes.

Tommy took no notice. 'But I'm a human...don't you want a demon as your deputy?' she said, in an oddly plaintive voice.

*Oh no, Tommy,* I thought, *don't fall for her charm.* If Lilith really did want Tommy as her deputy, there couldn't be a good reason for it.

But Tommy *was* falling for it. I could see it in the way her face flushed and an uncertain smile spread over her lips.

'Well, some humans are special,' said Lilith, smiling back warmly. 'And you know, once you're back on Earth, there's nothing to stop you visiting some old friends if you wished...'

I'd had enough. 'But you like it here, don't you, Tommy?' I said. 'I mean, you don't *really* want to go back to Earth, do you?'

Tommy looked at Lilith then at Lucifer, and I realised I'd put my foot in it. She couldn't answer without offending one of them. Luckily Dad came to the rescue.

'Now, now, stop bombarding the poor girl with questions.' He turned to Lilith and started telling her about some documentary he'd seen called *The Exorcist*.

Tommy frowned and played with her food. I wondered why Lilith was being so nice to a human. It was weird. After all, she spent all her time corrupting humans on Earth and getting them sent here. Well, if I was stuck at dinner with the snake I might as well try to get something out of her. But I couldn't think of a way to bring up the subject of Dantalion. 'Hey, remember your son who I sent to Purgatory?' Yeah, that wouldn't go across so well. I tried another tack.

'How long do you plan to stay in Hell?' I asked.

Lilith waved her hand airily. 'Oh, just until I've found myself a new deputy.' She threw a sideways glance at Dad. 'Unless I have a reason to stay longer.'

Oh no. Nope, nope, nope. 'But imagine all the things that might be going wrong without you! Um...not nearly enough humans being tempted! You don't want to let things get out of control.'

Lilith gave me an icy glare. 'I daresay my fiends can manage without me for just a few days,' she said evenly.

The serfs came and took our plates away, and an uneasy silence fell over the table. I jumped to my feet. 'Well, thanks for dinner. See you later, Dad. Lilith.'

Tommy stood up but instead of turning to leave, she smiled at Lilith. 'Thank you for letting me take part in your contest. I appreciate it.'

Lilith's face split wide into a grin. 'But of course, my dear, us girls must stick together, mustn't we?'

Out in the corridor I turned to Tommy. 'What was all that about? You're not really thinking about leaving, are you?'

She smiled, but her eyes were sad. 'Of course not. Only... only it's Plan B. In case things don't work out for me here.'

'Why wouldn't things work out?' Dammit. I wasn't going to beg her to stay.

But she just shook her head and started walking. 'Come on. We've got more important things to think about. Whatever happens, I want to get rid of this curse, for me

182

and my mum. Let's get to the art workshop.'

'You don't think it's weird that Lilith was being so nice to you? She hates humans normally.'

Her lip wobbled. 'Thanks a lot. She couldn't just like me 'cos I'm awesome, could she? No, there has to be some evil secret plot behind it all. No one could possibly just like me for me, could they? Maybe I *should* go somewhere I'm actually wanted, since everything here is either trying to kill me or telling me I suck.'

'Don't be stupid, no one said you su—'

But she stormed off along the corridor.

'I'll see you at the workshop!' I called after her. 'I just need to go and feed Bruce.'

'Fine.' She ran off down the stairs.

*Humans.*

Up in my room, Loiter was back in his hammock, throwing snacks in the air for Bruce. Bruce wasn't much good at catch. The floor was littered with bits of popcorn.

'Hello, Jinx, what's up? Dolly's getting along nicely, by the way. Took a message to my tailor this morning without getting lost.'

'Everything's terrible,' I said.

Loiter leant out of his hammock. 'Oh dear. What now?'

I told him all about Pandora's curse and Boozy and

183

almost getting toasted in the factory and how I was worried Tommy wanted to leave. 'Living with my evil stepmother in a fortress halfway up a mountain on Earth! What is she thinking?' I was seriously sulking by now.

Loiter looked thoughtful. 'Remember she was abandoned by her parents. She's bound to be touchy about anything that makes her feel like she doesn't belong.'

'But she just found out that her mum *didn't* abandon her!' I steamed. 'And of course she belongs! I threw her a big birthday party just to show her how much she belongs, remember? And now she wants to leave Hell when we've been nothing but nice to her!'

Loiter rubbed his nose with one long claw. 'Well, there *are* possibly demons trying to kill her. That kind of thing does tend to make a person feel unwanted, you know. And she's believed all her life that her mother abandoned her. Maybe she still doesn't quite believe she didn't. It's just a theory at this point.' He reached up with his feet and hung upside down from the rafters. 'I don't think she actually wants to leave Hell. She just wants to feel wanted.'

'It's all Lilith's fault,' I grumbled, 'charming Tommy and telling her how she should come and live with her in the Himalayas. Reminding her how she misses Earth.'

'And if Tommy misses Earth you would stop

her from returning?'

I sighed. 'Well, no, of course not. But Lilith—'

'Don't you think you're just a tiny bit obsessed with Lilith? I understand why you don't like her, but—'

Bruce chose that moment to land on my head and I couldn't help but laugh. 'Look, Tommy's waiting for me, I'd better go. See you later.'

'Don't do anything I wouldn't do,' said Loiter, turning back over to go to sleep.

'That'd be pretty hard, since you never do anything,' I mumbled as I left.

'I heard that!'

I smirked and hurried off to the art workshop. There I found Tommy hunched over the computer in the office with Rodin.

I flopped into a chair next to them, and tried to pretend like Tommy and I hadn't just argued. 'Any luck?' I asked casually.

Tommy sighed. 'Nope. Dozens of paintings and statues of Pandora, but none of them tell us anything new.'

I jumped up. 'I know! What about the Sorceress Queen of Sumer?'

'The who now?'

'Just try a search on her. She was the one who ordered the

box to be made. And she holds the key to the curse. After all, she's the one who laid it on Pandora and her bloodline. At least, according to the book I read in the library.'

Tommy narrowed her eyes. 'The book you mysteriously lost.'

I ignored her. 'Monsieur Rodin, would you mind?'

'Certainly, certainly.' He tapped at the keyboard, and the screen wobbled blankly for several long seconds. Finally a photo popped up.

'Only this one result, I am afraid,' said Rodin.

It was an ancient-looking terracotta vase with black

186

illustrations on it.

'Can you make it bigger?' asked Tommy.

Rodin tapped at the keyboard again and the picture on the vase zoomed closer.

'Is very good style for such an old piece,' said Rodin, tilting his head and peering at it, but I wasn't listening.

The text beneath the vase said 'Sorceress Queen of Sumer, taken from a villa in Eridu, circa 7000BC'. The painting on the vase was black and pointy, like old-fashioned Egyptian figures. Half a dozen people were bowing to a kohl-eyed, black-haired queen on a throne. It was much too basic to show who the woman was, and there was no name written anywhere. But what there was, was a box in front of the queen, with spirits flying out. Pandora's Box.

'Pfft,' I said. 'I hate to be a downer but that just looks like the queen putting all the evils into the box. It doesn't even tell us her name.'

Tommy drew in a breath. 'No, look.' She tapped on the top right-hand corner of the screen.

I looked. The queen's right hand was closing the box, but her left hand was twisted back over her shoulder. And just leaving her fingertips was a key. 'She's throwing away the key? Why?'

'Because she isn't closing the box at all. She's opening it!

Look at her face. She's smiling. Why would she be smiling if she was closing it? She'd be scared, or relieved, or satisfied. But not grinning. And she is definitely throwing that key away. And look at the way her right hand is positioned...her fingers are inside the lid. She's opening it, Jinx, I tell you!'

'Is good?' said Rodin.

'I don't know what it is, but it's new information,' I said. 'OK, so the queen not only laid the curse on Pandora, but she's also the one who opened the box. Which means the story I read is wrong. But I'm not sure how this helps us.'

Tommy tapped her chin. 'I'm not either, but at least it's something. Let's—'

The door to the office flew open and a fat grey demon rushed in, eyes bulging with fear. 'Evacuate! Evacuate! Escape from the Monster Research Lab!'

Tommy and I stared at each other in horror.

188

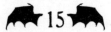

# 15

# The Opposite of Cute

TOMMY

RODIN FLEW OUT of the office into the art workshop, almost knocking over the grey demon, moving faster than I'd thought possible for a white-haired dead man. 'The art, the art! Shut the doors!'

'Stuff the art,' said Jinx as we all ran after him, 'save the living.'

'And the dead,' I reminded him.

A freakish hissing and screeching came from the hallway outside, like someone was murdering a violin. And a violinist. I skidded to a stop.

'What is it?' asked Jinx. 'A banshee? A kraken? A werewolf?'

The grey demon shook his head, looking so terrified that I wasn't sure I wanted to hear the answer. 'I don't know how it happened,' he panted, 'but someone let the cats out.'

I burst out laughing. '*That's* what you're all scared of? A bunch of fluffy kittens?'

He opened his mouth to reply, looked over my shoulder, then sprinted for the back of the room without a word. I spun round. Dozens of mewling kittens bounded into the room.

'Oh, come on!' I said. 'This is ridiculous. Why on earth would you be frightened of...' A tiny tabby opened its jaws like it was yawning. And yawning some more. The jaws gaped open so wide it was like the creature's head had split open – and within were three layers of needle-sharp teeth. It sank its fangs into the leg of one of the artists and blood sprayed the wall behind them. '...kittens.' I finished. 'Arrghhh!'

Jinx yanked my arm and we bolted away from the entrance towards the back of the room. I leapt at the nearest set of heavy metal shelves, kicking vases and figurines to the floor with a crash, and scrambled up it as fast as I could. Behind me Jinx flew into the air and landed on a shelf halfway up with a crunch.

I scooched along next to him and we gaped at the chaos enfolding in front of us. Two demon artists were flailing around in a whirlwind of fur and fangs and high-pitched screams. The rest had clambered up the shelves like us, and someone had locked themselves in the office. Rodin was trying to fight the killer kittens off with a broom.

'Now would be a really good time to tell me you've got a pile of throwing stars in your pocket,' said Jinx. 'Or a rocket launcher.'

'Never without them,' I said, pulling a hira-shuriken out of my hoody pocket. 'Well, not the rocket launcher bit. Not very portable. The bad news is I've only got two stars, and there are at least thirty baby monsters.'

Rodin seemed to decide that his art was not worth being mauled to death for after all, and ran back towards us and the safety of the shelves. At least, I presumed we were safe there. If they'd engineered the kittens to flip their heads open like swing-bins, for all I knew they could fly too. Two kittens were gaining on him. I took aim and spun a star at one, catching it full on and hurling it backwards in a fury of spitting and hissing. The second one dived at Rodin's shoe but he kicked it away and clambered up the stack of shelves next to us, puffing and panting.

I grimaced. 'If I ever had any doubt that I was cursed for all eternity... I tell you, if I ever meet that Sorceress Queen I am going to kill her so hard she'll be limping into Hell.'

Jinx stuck his jaw out. 'I am not having my tombstone saying "Death by Kittens",' he said. 'We have to do something.'

The kittens had finished dining on the two artists who

hadn't managed to escape. One poor demon gave a last twitch then fell still. Blood pooled across the floor.

I turned my last remaining throwing star round and round in my hand. 'Did anyone get out to sound the alarm?' I shouted across to Rodin.

He shook his head sadly. 'I do not think so. I see bodies in the 'allway.'

Jinx closed his eyes. 'Great.'

The kittens padded softly towards us, leaving red paw prints in their wake. With their jaws closed they looked cute, harmless, sweet. But the carnage around them was the opposite of cute.

'Dad and his brilliant schemes,' muttered Jinx.

I sighed. 'It's not your dad's fault. He warned us to stay away from that room. It's me. I'm jinxed.'

'Ha ha.'

'You know what I mean.'

By now the kittens were milling around the bottom of the shelves, mewling up at us, eyes wide. I stared down at them. 'Please don't be able to climb, please don't be able to climb,' I whispered. One tried to jump up to the first shelf, but it couldn't make it. I breathed a huge sigh of relief. 'They're too small.'

Another leapt up. It hung, swaying, from the first shelf by

its claws, then pulled itself up. The other kittens miaowed in victory and tried to follow it.

Jinx scrambled to his feet. 'Nope. Not too small. What now?'

I tried not to whimper. 'We're dead.'

'Speak for yourself.'

We scrabbled further up the shelves, the skritching of claws following us as we got higher and higher.

I grabbed a figurine of a demon and dropped it onto the nearest kitten but missed. My heart hammered in my chest. 'After everything I've survived I am not getting murdered by kittens,' I said.

Jinx's eyes suddenly grew wide. '*Rocket launcher,*' he said.

'Are you hallucinating or something? We don't have any rocket launchers. We don't have any tanks or bombs either. This is the art workshop, not the arsenal.'

'Monsieur Rodin!' he yelled. 'Your rocket, how does it work?'

Oh. *That* rocket.

Rodin's face lit up. 'Yes! The Art Rocket. It could work.' Then his face fell. 'But 'ow am I to reach it to make it work?'

'I can fly!' shouted Jinx. 'Just tell me how to do it!'

A kitten scrambled onto the shelf below me and I threw a paperweight of a dragon at it. The creature opened its jaws wide and roared at me. 'Hurry!'

'The switch is at the back, is labelled, is easy!' said Rodin. 'Switch on, press start!'

Jinx launched himself off the shelf and flapped across the room. The kittens paused in their climb and turned to watch him. Half of them were still milling about on the floor at the bottom of the shelves, too tiny to follow. The minute Jinx landed they ran at him and I screamed.

'Spray them! Spray them!'

Jinx flapped at the back of the brass drum and it began to spin. The kittens were almost on him now. He grabbed the nozzle and flew into the air just as a snarling furball snapped at his ankles.

'The black button! At the top!' shouted Rodin, sounding like he was about to burst.

Jinx slammed his hand down and all at once a gloopy spray of white foam whooshed out of the hose and landed on the mini monsters growling beneath him. Some tried to escape but they couldn't grab onto the slick floor with their claws. Jinx continued spraying until he had covered them all.

I threw my hands in the air. 'Yessss!'

Within seconds the plaster had set, and the floor was covered in what looked like tiny kitten figurines. I burst

out laughing. Then there was a hiss beneath me and a claw knifed into my toe. I yelped and threw my last remaining throwing star at the kitten clinging to my foot. Its head was sliced clean off its body and the headless kitten spun around, spattering me with blood. I screamed some more for good measure.

Then Jinx was dragging the hose over to us and spraying

195

the shelves with plaster, solidifying all the remaining kittens.

Ten minutes later, the attack of the killer kittens was over.

Jinx flopped to the floor and I hung my head in relief.

Rodin and the remaining artists cheered.

'Kittens,' I muttered. 'Is *nothing* safe in Hell?'

We left Rodin and his workers to clear up the mess and tell Lucifer about the mysterious break-out. After everything that had happened today all I wanted to do was dive face-first into bed. Jinx peered into the Monster Development Lab as we passed. The place was wrecked.

'How did they get out?' he said. 'Someone must have let them out. But...'

I grimaced at the bodies in the hallway. 'But it can't have been any of the demon scientists. They'd know better. At least, you'd think so.'

Jinx hurried on, looking queasy. 'Well, they do now.'

Upstairs, I followed Jinx into his room and sank into an armchair. 'That was fun.'

Bruce flapped in the window and landed on Jinx's shoulder. Jinx rubbed his head against him and sighed. 'I hate to say this, but I really do think you might be cursed. And when I say "might be"...'

'You mean definitely, a hundred per cent, curseder than a curseder thing.'

'Looks that way.' He flopped onto his bed. He shook his head and laughed quietly. '*Kittens*. I mean, seriously.'

'OK, so I wasn't kidding. That Sorceress Queen of Sumer is history.'

Jinx looked confused. 'Yes…?'

'No, I mean she's history, as in I am going to kill her in a thousand different ways. I am going to kill her so dead there aren't any pieces left to bury.'

'You are scary when you're angry. And what do you mean? I don't blame you for feeling like that, but she's very dead already.'

'Not a few thousand years ago, she isn't.'

He picked Bruce off his shoulder, stroked his wings and looked at me. 'Either I'm really tired, or you're making no sense at all.'

'You know The Waiting Room? You told me you used it when you went to stay with Dracula. Well, you can go back in time using it, right?'

Comprehension dawned in his eyes. 'Ahhh. You want to *actually* go back and kill the queen? To undo the curse?'

'Yes.'

'Except there's no way we'll get through The Waiting Room. The bureaucracy in that place is unreal. You need to file a visa just for one afternoon on Earth. And it's manned

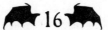

# Time is a Stack of Pancakes

### JINX

EARLY THE NEXT morning, me, Tommy, and a grumbling Loiter bundled into a rickshaw and headed out across Pandemonium.

'Could you *be* any more obviously off on a secret mission?' I said to Tommy.

She was dressed in black jeans with a black hood pulled over her blonde plaits, and was practically clanking with the weapon belt slung across her chest, which was groaning with throwing stars and knives and every kind of sharp pointy implement imaginable.

'I like to be prepared.'

I rolled my eyes. I wasn't a big fan of weapons. Not in a disapproving sort of way, obviously, being a demon. Just in a couldn't-hit-a-dreadbeast-at-fifty-paces-with-a-bazooka kind of way. All I had on me was a small knife a Bonehead called Sarika had once given me, and that was more a lucky charm. I was just going to have to rely on my wits – and quite possibly Tommy coming to my rescue.

Loiter yawned ostentatiously.

'You'll be back to bed in no time,' Tommy said, patting him on the arm.

Loiter growled and held up a paw. 'One,' he said, counting off on his claws, 'it's far too early for adventures. Two, even if it were later I don't *like* adventures. And three, I think this is a horrible plan and you're both going to wind up dead or stuck in ancient Sumer and then I'm going to have to come and rescue you which will *really* put a crimp in my day.'

'You *would* come and rescue us, though, wouldn't you? If we got stuck?' asked Tommy, picking at her nails and suddenly looking a lot less gung-ho.

'Absolutely not. So you should just call the whole thing off and let me go back to bed.'

The taxi swooped down and landed lightly in the courtyard in front of the Evil Eyrie. What Tommy had remembered was that The Waiting Room was not the only magical doorway to Earth's past. The Eyrie had a gateway too, for the messenger birds.

'How do you know it won't just be a zeegle-sized door?' I'd asked her.

'I don't. But we have to at least try. I can't go on like this. It's nerve-wracking, never knowing what's going to try to kill me next.'

I couldn't argue with that.

'Last chance to change your minds,' said Loiter.

I shook my head. 'Tommy's right. She's obviously cursed and we need to fix it before we all end up as cat food or the filling in a dreadmeat burger.'

Loiter looked curiously at us. 'It was really kittens?'

'Yup.'

'Your father has the strangest ideas sometimes.' He puffed his chest out. 'All right, then. Ready?'

'Yes,' said Tommy, looking fierce again. 'That Sorceress Queen is going to be sorry she was ever born.'

Loiter looked thoughtful. 'If you do actually succeed in killing her,' he said, 'I wonder if I'll be out of a job.'

'Huh?'

'Well, if it was this queen who loosed all the evils upon the world, if there *are* no evils, then, well...tricky for us demons. Not a lot to do.'

I gawped at him. 'I hadn't thought of that.'

'Then again,' he continued, 'the Earthly timeline doesn't like being altered. I expect it'd happen anyway, somehow or another.'

Tommy's face fell. 'Does that mean you don't think I can get rid of my curse?' she asked. 'I mean, that's changing the timeline too.'

'Oh no, I wouldn't worry about that. That's a small thing, and it only affects your bloodline. I don't see why that couldn't be changed.'

Tommy blew her cheeks out in relief, but Loiter hadn't finished.

'I *don't* think you can get rid of your curse, but that's because you're two small children on a fool's errand venturing into an unknown land plotting to kill the most highly protected citizen there.'

Tommy's relief melted into a pout.

Loiter strode off across the courtyard and we followed. He knocked on the door and, as planned, Tommy and I hid off to the side. After a few moments the door rattled and a feathery owl head popped out.

'Morning, Loiter!' said the zeegle meister. 'Bit early for you, isn't it? I'm just making breakfast – care for some sausages?'

'That,' said Loiter with feeling, 'is the best idea I've heard all day.' He stepped inside and the door swung shut behind them.

I counted to sixty then pushed open the front door an

inch and peeked through the gap. 'All clear,' I whispered to Tommy. We crept in. Voices and the clatter of crockery came from upstairs.

'There,' said Tommy, pointing at a fat iron ring embedded in the floor. She yanked at it and the trapdoor swung open easily without a sound, revealing a stone staircase. We hurried down it and pulled the trapdoor shut above our heads, leaving ourselves in pitch darkness.

'It would be a bit embarrassing to fall down the steps and die before we even leave the Eyrie,' I said.

'Hang on.' There was the soft rustle of Tommy searching her pockets, and then a gentle glow lit the darkness. Tommy held Sparky in her palm like a small torch.

'Hey, nice work, Sparky!'

The baby shocktopus illuminated a large vaulted cellar. At the far side, a round steel door the size of the trapdoor we'd come through was embedded in the wall.

'Not quite enough room to swing a cat, but enough for us to squeeze through,' said Tommy.

'Have you got any idea how you're going to get rid of Evil Witch Queen?' I said.

She waved her hand at me. 'We'll figure it out. One strange and complicated thing at a time. How do we work this machine?'

In The Waiting Room, there were two vast brass wheels which uniformed wheel-masters turned to choose a place and a date. Down here there were no staff or visas, but I was relieved to see that it was otherwise the same: two slightly smaller brass dials with markings hung from the stone wall. I ran my finger round the right hand one until I came to Eridu, then clicked the wheel round so it was at the top. 'What's the date?'

'What?'

I looked at Tommy. 'The date. *When* are we going to?'

'You were the one who read the book in the library.'

*Brimstone.* So I was. I tried to remember what it had said, but I had a sudden flashback to the staircase falling away beneath my feet and had to lean against the wall. 'About 7000BC, I think,' I said when I'd recovered.

'About?'

'Sorry. Ancient history books are a bit vague. But it said the Sorceress Queen reigned for over a century, so I'm sure we'll be fine.' I turned the dial on the second wheel all the way round to nine thousand years earlier.

'Good luck to us,' said Tommy.

'Because we always have such good luck,' I muttered.

'Wait!' said Tommy. 'How does time work when we go through this door? I mean, if we get lost and end up there for a week, is it a week in Hell too?'

'Oh yeah, I meant to tell you. Time doesn't work the same when we go through this door.'

She rolled her eyes at me.

'If you go to modern-day Earth, time works pretty much the same. But if you go back in history, time sort of telescopes. Loiter explained it to me once. The past is squished by all the future weighing down on it. Like a stack of pancakes. The further back you go, the less time will have passed when we get back. Since we're going all the way back to 7000BC, I reckon a week there will only be a few seconds here.'

'Time is a stack of pancakes.'

'Yes. It's very scientific.'

'Clearly. OK, let's do this.'

I turned the handle on the round door and we stepped through into the past.

We were in a small cave. Sunlight filtered through a crack in the rock. I shut the Eyrie door behind us and we slipped through the crack and found ourselves ankle-deep in sand.

'The past is hotter than I expected. Also windier,' said Tommy, brushing sweat from her forehead.

'Sumer was where Iraq is now,' I said. 'So, yeah.' I didn't like hot. Or deserts.

We struck out across the sand dunes, the cloudless blue sky looming down inconsiderately above us. There was nothing and no one in sight.

'Are you sure this is the right place?' asked Tommy. ''Cos this doesn't look much like a city to me.'

'Well, the gateways to Hell are hidden, so that means they aren't generally in the middle of a city,' I said. 'It won't be far.'

We huffed on through the desert, and up another huge dune. At the top, at last, I saw buildings in the distance. 'There it is! That must be Eridu.'

A sprawling collection of sand-coloured houses and temples stood in the distance, shimmering in the heat haze.

'It's...smaller than I imagined,' said Tommy. 'I thought this was a great city.'

So had I. I shrugged. 'Well, it'll be all the easier to find the palace. Come on.'

I slid down the slope and we trekked on sweatily.

'I hate sand,' grumbled Tommy. 'This reminds me of the Desert of Deception.'

'We're on Earth, there won't be any hellbeasts or sentient quicksand, don't worry.'

'I don't feel like I'm back on Earth. This all feels unreal.' She scratched her nose. 'I wonder what Ancient Sumerian people are like. I hope they don't worship cats. I've had quite enough felines for one week.'

As it turned out, cats weren't on the menu. Unfortunately, neither were Sumerians. We reached the gates of the city and looked around in dismay. The whole place was deserted and half-buried in sand.

'Oops,' I said.

'We're too late,' said Tommy. 'We must have got the dates wrong. This place looks like it's been abandoned for a hundred years.'

'Hellfire. We can go back to the Eyrie and change the

date, but we don't know when the Zeegle Meister might come down to the cellar to send a message. And if he catches us we won't have a chance to come back again.'

Tommy sat on a low wall and kicked her legs back and forth, looking frustrated. 'But I need to kill the queen. Or at least stop her from laying the curse on Pandora in the first place. A hundred years too late is as bad as nine thousand years too late.'

She was right. Why did nothing ever go easily for us? 'All right, come on, let's go back and try again.'

Tommy hopped off the wall and the Earth shook beneath my feet.

'Someone's been eating a lot of dreadbeast burgers lately,' I said.

'Ha ha.'

The ground shook again and a low rumbling like an earthquake sounded out. I spun round. 'What was that?'

Tommy shook her head, face pale. 'You promised no hellbeasts. Or quicksand.'

'Of course there aren't. It's probably a sandstorm or a tiny earthquake.' I turned away from Eridu and looked back the way we'd come. 'Let's just—'

A hump of sand sped towards us over the dunes.

Then another, and another, like vast tunnelling

earthworms. 'Uh...'

'Uh what?'

A black shiny head burst out of the sand and clattered towards us, tail swinging. In seconds the dunes in front of the city were crawling with black beasts the size of rickshaws, pincers snapping. *Giant sand scorpions.*

'I think I know why this place is deserted,' I said. 'Run!'

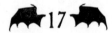

# The Hollow City

WE SWUNG ROUND and pelted back in through the city gates and down the wide boulevard that must once have been the main street.

'You...promised me...no...hellbeasts,' panted Tommy in between breaths.

'I'm not exactly thrilled about it either,' I yelled.

The scorpions scuttled through the gates and sped after us. We were probably the tastiest thing they'd seen in days. Tommy sprinted right down an alleyway and I followed. I looked desperately around for somewhere to hide but the sand had blocked all the doors and windows.

We took a right then a left and found ourselves in a sunken courtyard. Tommy stared wildly about. The telltale clack of pincers was right behind us. We were trapped. We backed away as three scorpions scurried into the courtyard, black eyes winking greedily.

'Oh no...Tommy, I can fly up. Can you get them

with your throwing stars?'

She yanked two out of her belt and hurled them at the nearest beast, but they just bounced off its hard carapace.

I cursed myself for being such a wimp. I could fly out of there, but I wasn't strong enough to carry Tommy more than a few feet.

'Maybe I could drop you on a rooftop and—'

Tommy vanished right before my eyes.

'Tommy!'

'Down here!' came a muffled voice.

The scorpions were only a few yards away now. I looked desperately all around me, took a step forward, and the ground beneath my feet gave way. I slid down and landed with a thump on a stone floor. Tommy stood in front of me, shaking sand out of her hair.

'Where are we?' I said.

'I dunno but let's get out of here before they follow us.'

Before us stretched a long corridor covered with blue and green mosaics. We ran down it but after a second I stopped and looked back.

'I don't think they're coming after us,' I said. 'Maybe they don't like being underground.'

'Or maybe they're just saving us for a snack later,' said Tommy, shaking more sand out of her clothes. 'I knew I hated deserts.'

'Sorry.'

'Never mind, let's just find a way out of here.' She took Sparky from a pocket and held him out in front of her again. We trod on nervously into the darkness.

'The buildings were only half-covered in sand,' I said. 'It shouldn't be too hard to find a way out, even if we have to dig a bit.'

Tommy swore about sand and deserts some more and I shut up.

The corridor opened out into a high-ceilinged chamber covered in more mosaics. It looked like the house of some rich person. Maybe this had once been the ballroom, or whatever Ancient Sumerians had instead of ballrooms.

'I hope this isn't some sacrificial chamber riddled with traps,' said Tommy. 'Hang on, look! There's daylight coming from up there.' She pointed far above our heads.

A tiny ray of sunlight struggled through a high window.

'Do you think you could carry me that far?' she asked.

'I can try.'

'Do or do not, there is no try,' she said. 'If you drop me from that height I'll be strawberry jam.'

In one corner the sand was piled up into a mini-dune. 'Let's see if we can climb up there and get a bit nearer.'

Over by the wall even more sunlight beamed down, illuminating the room. Tommy slipped Sparky back into a pocket in her belt and shut the clasp. 'All right. Here's hoping there are no giant sand scorpions waiting for... Look at that!' She pointed at one of the mosaics on the wall in front of us. 'Doesn't that look like...'

'*Pandora.*'

The mosaics formed a mural, like a comic strip, one picture beside the other. The one Tommy had spotted showed a yellow-haired woman hammering at a box. Beyond her, a familiar-looking cave glowed red in the distance. The next showed a dark-haired queen holding the finished box up over her head, while all around her kohl-eyed subjects cheered.

Tommy bounced up and down. 'Maybe this shows how she laid the curse on Pandora! Maybe it can even tell us how to break it! Quick, help me.' She started scrabbling away at the drifted sand that was covering the rest of the mosaic. I dug along with her. Ten minutes and one ripped fingernail later, we had uncovered the next mural. I gasped.

The Sorceress Queen sat on a throne in her palace. But instead of subjects before her, as in the previous picture, what it showed was snakes. Lots and lots of snakes.

213

Tommy and I stared at each other. The Sorceress Queen was *Lilith*.

'You were right all along,' said Tommy. 'She *was* up to something.'

But I didn't feel very happy about it. 'So she opened the box and framed Pandora for it. But why commission the box in the first place?'

'Maybe Lilith just needed a way to transport all the evils from Hell to Earth?' said Tommy. 'What if the box was never meant to keep the evils safe? It was just a demonic suitcase. Maybe she planned to set them free from the beginning.'

'A demonic suitcase.'

'For that nice relaxing weekend break in Hell.'

'Destroying humanity, all-inclusive.'

Tommy snorted.

I rubbed my nose. 'So...what? Afterwards, she decided to hang out pretending to be an Earthly queen for a bit longer?'

'Remember when we overheard her and your dad talking in the dining room? He was saying she always preferred Earth to Hell.'

'And she said the humans treated her like a queen. I thought it was just a figure of speech.'

'So, she liked hanging out on Earth lording it over humans. But if she wanted to stay, she'd need someone to blame, so her subjects didn't blame her. But why curse Pandora? Pandora did exactly what she was supposed to do.'

Tommy scowled. 'Except die. Lilith needed her to die and take the truth with her.'

'Didn't do a very good job, leaving behind incriminating murals.'

'Maybe the mural was done after Lilith had left, after

everyone knew the truth about who she really was. Or maybe she just had a party with snakes.' Tommy slumped against the wall. 'So much for Plan B...' she said with a sigh.

'What are you talking about?'

'I thought she liked me. Lilith. I really thought she liked me.'

'I'm sorry.'

'It's OK. You can say I told you so.'

'Wait! If it's Lilith, maybe there's no curse after all. Remember when we first met? I thought you suddenly wanting to set the lion on your uncle sounded like the work of fiends. Come to think of it, your mum hearing voices sounds like it could be fiends too.' I beamed at her. 'Tommy! What if the book was wrong? *What if there was never a curse?* What if it was Lilith and her fiends all along?'

She shoved off from the wall, her face lighting up. *'No curse,'* she repeated slowly. 'That would be amazing! But... Do you think Lilith has spent thousands of years sending fiends to get revenge on every single one of Pandora's descendants? That sounds like way too much effort, even for a serious grudge.'

'So why was she after you and your mum? If it

wasn't to do with Pandora?'

She shrugged. 'No idea. No, it *has* to be something to do with Pandora—'

My eyes grew wide. 'The box! What about Pandora's Box?'

'What about it?'

'What if Lilith wants it?'

Tommy pointed at the mural. 'But she had it.'

'That was thousands of years ago. Maybe she lost it.'

'It's a bit big to lose down the back of the sofa.'

'Very funny. Seriously, what if she lost it, or it was stolen, and she's been trying to get it back all this time? What if, I don't know, it has magic evil powers or something? Something to help her take over Hell?'

Tommy frowned. 'But *I* don't know where the box is.'

'But maybe you don't need to know. Maybe Lilith already knows where it is...but she can't get to it herself. What if the box was in Hell all along?'

Tommy punched the air. 'The contest!'

'What about it?'

'I just remembered what the next trial is.'

'And...?'

'A treasure hunt. It's a treasure hunt.'

*Percival was not worried. He was not alarmed. No, Percival was freaking out. He didn't care if that sounded desperately unfiendish, it was the truth. Just when things had been going so well – demon kids failing trials left and right, Alethea smiling at him three times now – he had realised who the child was.*

*Lilith had mentioned a Bonehead in passing, of course. Someone who was staying in Darkangel Palace. As bizarre and inappropriate as Percival found this idea, he hadn't given it much thought. Until she'd walked right up to him and told him her name. The Bonehead sleeping under the King of Hell's very roof was none other than Tomasina Covelli. And that name did not bring back happy memories for Percival.*

*'This is most unusual,' he had told Lilith, that Earthly Monday ten months ago.*

*'I know it's unusual, Percival, I'm not an idiot,' she'd snapped. 'Just do what you're told.'*

*And so he had.*

*What he had done, for the first time in his 2039 years, was send fiends off to corrupt a child. But he hadn't been happy about it. Not because he had any sort of conscience when it came to human children – he didn't – but because if this all went horribly wrong he knew exactly who'd get the blame from Lucifer, and it wasn't his gorgeously evil ex-wife.*

*And now his biggest secret was staring him right in the face. Percival wasn't good with secrets. They made him break out in a rash. He was a fiend, after all, evil was his business, and he was surrounded by hundreds of others in that same business. There wasn't usually any need for lies, not between themselves. The lies were reserved for the humans.* Wouldn't you be happier if you were richer? Then why not put the rent up on the blocks of flats you own? Wouldn't it be nice not to have anyone yelling at you any more? Think of the peace and quiet if you poisoned your husband. Want to be prime minister? Pay a few bribes, no one will ever know.

*And the one he would never forget – even though he hadn't been there himself and had only read it in the report afterwards:* He's such a horrible man. If you just pulled the lion's ears you wouldn't have to put up with him any more.

If I get out of this mess in one piece, *he swore,* I will never break the rules ever, ever again.

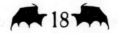

# A Match Made in Hell

## TOMMY

'SO IF LILITH and her fiends were to blame for sending you to Hell all along,' said Jinx, floorboards creaking as he paced up and down his bedroom, '– not your uncle, or some stupid curse – that means this whole contest was a smokescreen too. Lilith arranged it all just so you could get Pandora's Box for her.'

After a nervous and sweaty run across the rooftops of Eridu and the sand dunes of Sumer, and a relieved rickshaw ride back to the palace, we were back in Darkangel Palace, trying to decide what to do next. Sparky, who was apparently as fond of sand as I was, was taking revenge by trying to burn a hole through the windowpane.

'It's not paranoia when everyone's really out to get you,' I grumbled. 'As far-fetched as it sounds, it makes sense. It'd explain why I found the trials so easy. She wanted me to win. Maybe she knew Loiter would help me with the Eyrie...'

'And the riddles were a piece of cake.'

'Even the whole evil mirror twin thing, while creepy as heck...now that I think about it, I was never really in any danger.'

'Plus it explains why she was trying to put people off by telling us how dangerous it was.'

I smirked. 'Worked on you.'

'Because sensible people avoid the danger.'

'But why would the box be in Hell in the first place?' I said, sitting on the desk and swinging my legs back and forth. 'And if it is in Hell, surely Lilith could get to it.'

'I don't know. Maybe Pandora hid it here? I know of at least two legends of humans who entered and left Hell while they were still alive.'

'Seems unlikely.'

'It does. But if Lilith had put it here, like you said, she'd be able to get to it.'

'So...Pandora hid the box in Hell. But she somehow cast some sort of spell so Lilith couldn't get to it? Or maybe there's some giant hellbeast protecting it or something.' I puffed my cheeks out. 'Ugh, hellbeasts. I think we've reached the point where we need to go and tell your dad about all this.'

Jinx shook his head. 'And say what? That several thousand years ago Lilith put on a sparkly crown and hung out with mortals for a bit? With her custom-made demonic suitcase? That we have some vague hunches about fiends? We don't have proof for any of it.'

'But you heard her mention Dantalion. Though I guess that doesn't prove anything either.'

'I wish it did, but it's still not enough. You saw what Dad was like, all *ha ha, my adorable ex-wife who eats entire cities*. He'll think we're kicking up a fuss over nothing. Plus he thinks you're in Hell because of your uncle, and he doesn't like to be wrong. He can be quite vain.'

I swore a bit and kicked a bookshelf. 'All right, so what do I do? Keep taking part in *Hell's Got Talent*? But then I'm just doing what Lilith wants me to do. The minute I find the box, she'll take it from me and do whatever evil things she's planning to do with it. Which are probably going to be very bad news for everyone.'

'We still don't definitely know she wants you to find the box. This is all a theory based on that mural.'

'But it makes sense. Especially if there's something in the box.'

He sighed. 'It does. So...just stop taking part in the contest. She can't force you to, not with Dad around.'

I ran my hands through my hair. 'But if I don't find the box for her, I can guess what she'll do. She'll try to get my mum sent to Hell and use her to find it. Or she'll just force me to do it somehow anyway. No, what we have to do is find Pandora's Box first. And destroy it.'

A stink of melted glass wafted through the room. I plucked Sparky off the window and put him on the desk. '*Percival*,' I said. 'He's the one running things. He'll have all the info about the contest. What we need to do is steal his itinerary, skip the next place on the list and go straight on to the last trial. That's bound to be where the box is. We go there, destroy it, end of story.'

'Destroy an unbreakable box.'

'We'll find a way.'

'An unbreakable box which maybe has the most evil of all evils still in it.'

'If you don't stop being Captain Doom I'm going to reconsider your worth as a sidekick.'

'Hey! You're the sidekick, I'm...Batman.'

'Please. You're totally Robin.' I pointed at the weapons belt stretched across my chest. '*I'm* Batman.'

Jinx stuck out his chin. 'But *I'm* a prince of Hell...' I whipped two throwing stars out and waved them at him. '...who would prefer to keep his nose. Fine. I'll be... Spider-Man. OK, so that could work. But Lilith can't know we're on to her. We can't get caught. So we have to get

Percival out of the way first.'

'I think I know how to do that,' I said, feeling mischievous for the first time in far too long.

Alethea squeaked. 'Really? He wants to meet me?'

'Totally,' I said, trying not to gag at the stench of dragon poop.

Alethea flung open the stable door and bounced up and down.

'At the Sin-e-max at eight,' said Jinx. 'They're showing *How to Train Your Dragon.*'

'Oh, how sweet of him!' trilled Alethea.

Sweet was the absolute last word I'd use to describe Percival, with his translucent skin, twig-like body and comb-over, but there was no accounting for taste. And we needed to get him out of his room. Jinx had pretended he'd needed to send Percival a message and had asked one of the palace's grey messenger demons which room he was staying in. We'd already slipped a flowery note under his door signed 'Alethea', asking him to come and see the film with her. The way I'd caught him looking dreamily at her I was pretty sure it was a cinch.

'Very sweet,' I said, through gritted teeth. 'Have

a lovely time!'

'Oh, thank you so much!' She looked down at her filthy clothes. 'I've got to go and find something to wear!' And she dashed off in the direction of the servants' quarters.

At half past seven, Jinx and I were hanging over the staircase in the East Wing where Lilith and her entourage of fiends were staying. Lilith, of course, had the penthouse suite, which was lucky for us. The fiends were several floors below. Now we just needed Percival to take the bait.

'What if he doesn't want to go on a date with Alethea?' said Jinx.

'Are you kidding? I saw the way he looked at her.'

Jinx snorted. 'A match made in Hell. Especially considering how they both stink.'

I elbowed him in the ribs. 'Shut up, I like Alethea.'

'Yeah, me too. She has terrible taste in demons, though.'

I couldn't argue with that.

Just as my legs were starting to go numb from kneeling on the cold stone floor, a door slammed beneath us and Percival walked into the lobby below, carrying a box of chocolates. His comb-over was slicked neatly across his head. He stopped in front of the doors leading outside, took a deep breath, and squared his shoulders.

'Aww, he's nervous,' I said.

Then he opened the door and was gone.

Two minutes later Jinx and I were inside his room.

'Eww,' I said. The smell of brimstone hung in the air like rotten eggs. 'This is even worse than your bedroom.'

'Very funny.' Jinx was already at the desk, opening and closing drawers. 'Got it!'

I bent my head over the paper as he ran his finger down the itinerary.

Thugsday, Noon
Trial Five: Resourcefulness
Object: Find a toaster
Time allotted: 24 hours
Location: The Clocktower
Notes: Any pupil smart enough to still be in the contest should know to go to the White Market to find Earthly items

'That sounds easy, again. Like they want you to succeed,' said Jinx.

'Yup. Although that means other people could succeed too.'

226

'But there are only about twelve of you left. And maybe it doesn't matter, because maybe only someone descended from Pandora – i.e. *you* – could complete the final trial anyway.'

'Yeah, maybe.'

We read on.

Fienday, Noon
Trial Six: Resourcefulness
Type: Treasure Hunt
Object: Find the Unbreakable Box
Time allotted: 24 hours

Location: The Devouring Sands
Notes: Classified

Jinx punched the air. 'We were right! The Unbreakable Box has to be our missing demonic suitcase. And if we skip the next trial, we've got a day-and-a-half head start. Brilliant!'

But my stomach was heaving. I prodded the piece of paper. 'Um, Jinx, what are the Devouring Sands?'

'Well they're sort of like quicksand, but they're infused with magic so when you get sucked through you end up beneath Hell in... Oh.'

I threw my hands in the air. 'More sand! Why me?' I leant back against the desk and stuck my bottom lip out.

'Gah,' said Jinx. 'But you can't drown in the Devouring Sands, honest, they're just a gateway.'

I narrowed my eyes. 'You said there wouldn't be any hellbeasts in Sumer either.'

'Well, technically they weren't hellbeasts...' He trailed off as I glared at him.

'And what's so dangerous or special it needs to be hidden beneath a gateway like that anyway?'

'It's...look, we'd better not hang around here. Even with Percival gone, someone else might come in – you never know. Let's go.'

'Wait a sec, what about this bit – *Notes: Classified*? We should have a look for anything marked classified. Might help.'

We searched the remaining desk drawers, a chest of drawers, and a particularly smelly wardrobe, and rifled through the books in the bookcase. I even looked under the mattress. But there were no classified notes to be found.

'Maybe Lilith hasn't even told the fiends what she's really up to,' said Jinx, rubbing his eyebrow. 'Maybe only she knows the classified information.'

'Oh no.' I shook my head violently. 'We are not going poking around Lilith's room.'

He held his hands up. 'I am entirely with you on your complete cowardice on that one.'

'Good.'

We tidied the room up quickly, making sure it was just as we'd left it, read the itinerary once more to make sure we hadn't missed anything, then left the fiends' quarters in a hurry.

'Burglary achieved!' said Jinx with a grin as we ran back up to our floor.

But I was remembering the quicksand in the Desert of Deception, sucking at my shoulders and trying to drag me down into its depths. I felt short of breath just thinking about it. When we got to Jinx's room I dashed through it, yanked open a window and leant out, taking a deep breath.

Jinx came and sat beside me on the window seat.

'☠♥♦♦♀  ♦♣←♥☎  Ⓨ☎←♂,' said a scratchy voice.

I looked down and saw Grrr and Arrg grinning up at me. 'Hello, boys! What've you been up to?'

Arrg gave me a skullish grin. '♀☎  ☎♦♦♣  ☎♣☀Ⓨ☎☀Ⓨ ♀♦♣ ' he said, hanging upside down from the window frame.

I smirked and turned back to Jinx. 'So our crackpot theory was right. Lilith definitely set this whole thing up just to get to Pandora's Box.'

'And you're the lucky Chosen One.'

'Hmph. I always thought being a Chosen One would be glamorous. That there'd be parades and medals. Distinct lack of glamour so far.'

'If we get out of this alive I promise to organise you a parade. With glitter cannons and marching bands and lots of people sucking up to you.'

'I want dragons too.'

'A parade with dragons. Deal.'

I sighed. 'So, I really don't want to hear about it, but I guess I need to. Tell me more about these Devouring Sands.'

He leant back against the window and waved at Grrr

and Arrg. 'Like I said, it's just a gateway. It won't hurt you.'

'And you know this because you've used this gateway lots of times before, right?'

'Um...not so much.'

'Jinx, have you *ever* used it?'

'Not in so many words.'

I rolled my eyes. 'All right, so when we go through this perfectly safe weird Hellish gateway that you've never used before, where do we come out?'

Jinx looked out of the window and mumbled something that sounded like 'the flat cake'.

'The what now?'

He turned back to me but couldn't quite look me in the eye. 'The Black Lake.'

'And this Black Lake is obviously a happy, fun sort of place full of bunnies and rainbows, right?'

'You know the river Lethe?' he asked.

I shook my head.

'In Earth myths, it's the river of forgetting that flows through the Greek underworld. Except it isn't a myth. It actually exists, here in Hell, beneath the city.'

'OK....'

'Souls once came to Hell along the river. But memories don't just vanish. All the memories of the dead were sucked into the river and came to rest where it ends: the Black Lake.'

'So not so much bunnies and rainbows.'

'Not so much.' He shrugged. 'I mean, I've never actually been there. But it's supposed to be a very, very dangerous place.'

'Memories are dangerous?'

'The wrong ones, yes. They can suck you in and never let you out again.'

'Great.'

'But it'd make sense to hide Pandora's box there. It'd be hard to get to. From what I learnt in school, the Black Lake is at the centre of an enormous underground cave system. So the box could be anywhere.'

'So it could take us days to find it? By which time Lilith will have finished with the next trial?'

'Um.'

'You really suck at morale building, you know that?'

'Sorry.'

I'd survived zeegles and spikemoths and giant scorpions and my evil mirror twin over the past few days, but I had a sinking feeling those were going to be nothing compared to whatever lay beneath the Devouring Sands.

My evil twin. I thought again about what the doppelganger had said: *Without them, you're nothing.*

What was more, now we were safely out of reach of giant scorpions and killer kittens, I'd realised it was Thugsday. Which meant Persephone would be home tomorrow. Like I needed something else to worry about. If it wasn't one evil queen out to get me, it was another.

'Jinx, when your mum comes home...'

'Yes?'

'Do you think you could—'

There was a massive crash and Argg flew straight through the window, sending glass flying everywhere. Jinx and I jumped backwards. 'What the Hell?'

More sounds of breaking glass and crashing came from outside. Grrr smashed through what was left of the window. '⍨♦☙ ☙θ☙ θ☰ ☎♦←♦ ' he shouted.

'What's happening?'

He gabbled something in Gargoylish, too fast for me to understand.

'What did he say?' I asked Jinx, who was already pulling me out of the room.

'Someone's put a spell on him. He's not in control. Him and all the other palace gargoyles are being made to smash up the palace, and everyone in it. It's got to be Lilith. Come on, we need to get out of here!'

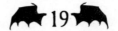

# 19

# The Bone Quarry

JINX

WE FLEW DOWN the stairs, chaos everywhere as demons and serfs ran this way and that, trying to escape the gargoyles.

I clenched my fists. 'How dare Lilith put a spell on the gargoyles! They'd never hurt a fly normally,' I fumed as we ran.

An alarm like a repeating foghorn boomed out, over and over.

'What in the shiny blue heck is she up to?' huffed Tommy.

'Search me.'

We skidded down the main stairs and out of the palace. Looking up I saw most of the windows were shattered and dozens of gargoyles were slamming into the building, raining rock down everywhere. Shrieks and screams came from inside.

'Whatever she's up to, seems like destroying the box is even more urgent,' I said.

Tommy nodded. 'Let's go.'

We dashed over the bridge that arched high over the fiery moat, hailed a rickshaw and flew off to the Devouring Sands.

I hated to leave the palace, but Dad would know what to do. He'd get the situation under control.

'Wait,' said Tommy, 'let's go and get Loiter. Please?'

I thought for a second. 'Do we really want to drag him into this mess?'

'A powerful demon who can shoot fire from his fingertips? Absolutely.'

'Yeah, I don't know what I was thinking.' I tapped the driver on the shoulder and asked him to go to the Pale Pastures and step on it.

It was dark now, and the city spread out below us, the white veins in the marble glowing gently like fairy lights. It was eerily beautiful. If it hadn't been for the screams of terror coming from behind me.

'So how do we get into the sands?' asked Tommy. 'Will they be guarded?'

'No. Well, not unless Lilith has sent some of her fiends there. People don't actually want to go to the Black Lake. No need to guard something that isn't sought after.'

'That is both good news...and quite terrifying.'

'Yeah.'

We skidded to a stop in front of Loiter's house. I jumped out and banged on the door. Silence. I banged harder. Finally a big ball of fur came swooshing down the glass slide and the door swung open. 'Thank the dark lords,' said Loiter. 'So you survived Ancient Sumer?'

'Just,' said Tommy, with a scowl.

I hurriedly told him about Lilith and the mosaic and the gargoyles attacking Darkangel Palace. 'So will you come with us and help us destroy Pandora's Box?' I finished, out of breath.

Loiter looked the angriest I'd ever seen him. 'How dare she trick a child into being sent to Hell? I'm so sorry, Tommy. Not to mention enchanting the gargoyles. When I get my hands on her...'

'I'll take that as a yes.'

'Too right. I'll meet you in the Bone Quarry.' He vanished in a flash of amber light.

The rickshaw took off again and Tommy crossed her arms. 'I probably shouldn't ask, but what's the Bone Quarry?'

'Please don't threaten me with spiked objects, but I don't know. I guess it's whatever's beneath the Devouring Sands.'

'I thought the Black Lake was beneath them?'

'Well, not directly beneath. We have to find it.'

She held her hands up like she was about to strangle me then yelped. 'Gargoyles!'

I spun round and looked back at the palace. Half a dozen gargoyles were following our cab. 'Oh no. Driver, could you hurry it up a bit please?'

The driver flapped faster and then began to descend.

Tommy let out a gasp. 'That's the Devouring Sands?' she said, eyes wide. 'That is not at all what I expected.'

Below us spread out a vast amphitheatre, twenty stages of circular rock with seats cut into them, surrounding a sandy centre. The rickshaw drifted down onto the top layer. I looked back and saw the gargoyles drawing nearer. I stuffed a five-demonius note into the driver's hand and ran down the steps, Tommy beside me.

'Yeah,' I puffed. 'This used to be a sports stadium. Of sorts.'

'Like Roman gladiators?'

'Yep. Boneheads or sometimes demons who'd got into trouble fought each other, or sometimes hellbeasts. But the thing was they had to fight the landscape too.'

Tommy grimaced as we thumped down the aisle. 'So is this all quicksand? Does all of this suck you down to the cave system below? Must have been pretty short fights.'

'No, that's the thing. Only part of it is quicksand, a few metres by a few metres. At least, that's what Loiter told me once. I'm too young to remember it being open. And what made the battles so exciting is that the gateway moved around.'

'Much as I never in my life wanted to step onto quicksand again, that's terrible news. How are we going to know which part of the stadium to go to? This place is huge.'

'We aren't. Sorry.' I looked up at the sky. 'But we're going to have to find it quickly. We've got company.'

Tommy looked vaguely green. 'We just run around till we get sucked through quicksand to a Hellish underworld? Or else get battered to death by gargoyles?'

'Yup, pretty much.'

'We do have *such* adventures, don't we?' she said through gritted teeth.

I pelted down the steps and skidded to a halt at the bottom of the amphitheatre. The palace emergency alarm boomed in the distance, but the sands blew lazily around before us in utter silence. There were no lights down here, only a handful up on the top row. I could barely see a thing.

The gargoyles were at the top of the stadium now. Tommy stepped gingerly onto the sand. I ran off all over like a pinball trying to find the magic gateway. I didn't know what sort of damage a solid stone gargoyle could do, but I wasn't in any hurry to find out. Then I tripped over a rock and fell straight onto the sand. And *into* the sand.

'Tommy! Over here! I've found—' I swallowed a mouthful of sand as I was sucked down. I shut my eyes and lips tight and felt a hand grip mine. I really hoped it was Tommy and not a gargoyle.

The hand gripped my wrist so hard it felt like it would shatter any minute. We plunged down and down. I tried not to struggle, thinking the journey would go quicker if I didn't, but I could feel Tommy beside me, flailing and kicking her legs. Or maybe it *was* a gargoyle trying to attack me. Just as I was starting to go light-headed from holding my breath, I felt my ankles kick free and then we were falling through space, and the next thing I knew we'd landed upside down in a sand dune.

I opened my eyes to a frantically shaking Tommy, her eyes still tight shut.

'Hey, look, it's OK, we made it. You can open your eyes now.'

We had landed in a heptagonal room, the floor covered with sand dunes, every inch of the walls studded with... skulls. Charming. A whispering noise seemed to come from them, like paper being rubbed together. The Bone Quarry. Of course. Some of the skulls had lit candles in them, which cast an eerie glow across the floor. Seven exits led off. I looked up. Only a few feet above our heads, the Devouring Sands rippled up and down like waves.

Tommy opened her eyes one at a time, her breath coming in huge, shuddering gasps. 'I...I suddenly thought, right in the middle of all that sand...I thought what if this gateway only opens for demons? What if the magic doesn't work on Boneheads and I'm stuck there for ever and ever...' She swallowed a sob and I hugged her until she stopped shaking.

'All right?' I asked.

'All right.' Her eyes widened as she took in the décor. 'Skulls. Yippee.'

'You are massively brave and I'm sorry you had to go through that. On the bright side, you never have to do it again.'

'Except...we don't actually know how to get out of here, do we?'

'Well, not exactly. But if this was Lilith's last trial there has to be a...' I suddenly realised the flaw in that theory.

'Except the whole contest was just for show. She probably didn't care if I got out alive, as long as I got Pandora's box for her. No, but wait, Lilith – or whoever she sent to pick up the box – would need a way out.'

'Er...'

She narrowed her eyes. 'Er what?'

'Lilith is as old as my dad. So she can do that whole instant beaming up from one place to another thing, same as Loiter. She doesn't need an exit.'

For a second I thought Tommy might start crying. Or murder me. Instead she raised a finger. 'Hang on.' She popped open a pocket on her Weapon Belt of Doom, and pulled out Sparky.

'You brought Sparky?' I said, slightly taken aback.

'I wasn't going to leave him alone in the palace when it was under attack. Plus you never know when you might need to know what's true or false.'

'Ah. Good plan. So?'

She turned to the tiny shocktopus. 'There is another exit from these caves.'

Nothing happened.

Her head fell forward. 'Oh, thank heavens. He didn't shock me. So there is a way out. Somewhere.'

That was the first good news we'd had in ages. 'Awesome.'

Tommy coughed. 'Let's get out of here. It's creeping me out having that sand over my head, like it all might fall down any minute.'

There was a burst of orange light and I covered my eyes with my hand. An angry sloth appeared in front of us.

'Loiter, you made it!'

He squared his shoulders. 'Too right I did. Where to?'

'I was hoping you'd know.'

'Sorry. Never had any cause to come down here before.'

Tommy and I ran around the cave, peering into each of the entrances. Two were blocked by rock falls, but that still left five other exits, all of which led into gloomy corridors, also embedded with skulls.

Tommy squeaked as a flaxitt ran out of a corridor over her foot.

'Let's take that one,' I said.

'What? No. Intelligent people go away from the scaly, beady-eyed vermin, not towards them.'

'But if beady-eyed vermin are coming from that direction,' said Loiter, 'that means it's probably not blocked further down. It has to lead somewhere.'

'Have I told you lately how much I don't like you?' grumbled Tommy. But she followed us down the corridor.

Several more flaxitts scuttered past us and I could feel Tommy staring daggers at my back as we crept on. The papery whispering grew louder as we headed deeper underground, sending shivers up my spine. The air smelled of dust and death.

Finally, to my relief, we came out into a huge circular room, surrounded by pillars that reached high above our heads. It had the same tasteful grinning skull décor, and the whispering was now loud enough to hear words. Or rather word.

'*Damned,*' hissed the skulls, over and over. '*Damned damned damned.*'

'Tell me something I don't know,' said Tommy, rolling her eyes.

I smirked. 'Glad to see you're back to your old self.'

'I really think your dad should get a new decorator. Goth is *so* over.'

A soft thud echoed out and I spun round, but couldn't see anything. 'Also better lighting,' I muttered.

The three of us stopped in the middle of the room and looked around, but there were no exits at this end except the one we'd come through. Another soft thud, hardly loud enough to hear over the whispering.

'Did you hear that?' asked Loiter.

I nodded. But as far as I could see there was no one in the room except us. We continued to head through the hall of skulls.

'What would be nice would be a big sign saying "Black Lake This Way", said Tommy.

'Now that you mention it...' I pointed to the far side of the room. A massive set of double doors stood beneath a carved archway. On the archway were written the words 'Abandon All Hope Ye Who Enter Here'.

'Oh, goody,' said Tommy. 'I've really missed those signs.' She jogged over towards the door.

I went to follow but caught my ankle and stumbled. I looked down...at which point it's possible I might've screamed a bit.

A snake was trying to coil round my ankle. I kicked it away, but then I saw another. And another. I looked up and saw snakes slithering out of the mouths of skulls all over the walls.

'Loiter! Little help here!' But Loiter was nowhere to be seen. Oh no. 'Uh, Tommy. We have a problem.'

I yanked the dagger out of my pocket and lashed out

at the nearest snakes. Tommy hurled a throwing star and sliced the head off a huge cobra. But more and more just appeared.

'Where's Loiter?' she yelled.

'I don't know. Maybe he's gone to get help?' But Loiter could've fought off a few snakes. Why would he leave us right when we needed him? It didn't make sense.

Tommy and I took one look at each other and ran for the doors. But they wouldn't open.

'They're jammed or locked,' huffed Tommy, pulling on them with all her might. We backed up against them. The entire floor was now a writhing, hissing carpet of snakes. Suddenly I was yanked off my feet and dragged along the ground. I smacked my head on the floor and cried out in pain. Tommy stamped at the snakes and threw tiny daggers and stars at them but each time she killed one, another appeared. The snakes dragged me across the room and this was it, I was going to die, I was so going to die, why hadn't I just told Dad about all this, why hadn't I brought more weapons why... Why weren't the snakes trying to bite me?

There was a thud as Tommy was also overrun with snakes and pulled to the ground. She yelled and struggled but they wound around her wrists and ankles until she, like me, couldn't move.

A flash of blue hellfire lit up the hall like daytime. I blinked. Had Loiter come back to rescue us? Or even Dad? The light had blinded me and I shook my head to clear my vision. Then I heard a voice.

'Hello, children,' said Lilith. 'Decided to come to the party early?'

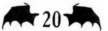

# 20

# Row, Row, Row Your Boat, and Try Not to Scream

TOMMY

LILITH TOWERED OVER me and Jinx as we lay on the floor, wrapped in snakes, unable to move a muscle. Her dark hair was loose and she wore black jeans and a jumper, as if she were just popping out for brunch. Her face split into a grin as wide as a Halloween pumpkin.

Well, this was very not good.

I glared at her.

'Aren't you going to ask how I knew you were here?' she said, the merest hint of irritation in her voice.

'Is this the part where you give us the evil villain speech and explain everything you're up to?' I said, faking a yawn. I was done being scared. The Devouring Sands had taken the last ounce of terror I had left.

Her eyes narrowed. 'Your ever-so-friendly gargoyles were kind enough to eavesdrop for me.'

'Because you cast a spell on them,' I said. 'They couldn't help it. We know it was you who set them loose on the palace.'

'But why?' said Jinx.

Lilith waved her hand nonchalantly. 'Just a little distraction. Something to keep your father busy while I attend to business down here.'

Jinx glared daggers at her. 'And we know it was you who

sent Tommy to Hell. I bet you set the kittens loose, too, didn't you?' Then he shook his head. 'But why would you try to kill Tommy? You need her to get Pandora's Box.'

Lilith smiled. 'What makes you think I was trying to kill *Tommy*?'

Jinx gulped. 'Why would you want to kill me?'

'Do you remember a brother of yours called Dantalion? Or should I say half-brother? My son? *My son whom you sent to live the rest of his days in Purgatory?*'

'He started it.'

'You could've killed me too!' I said. 'Wait, did you set the dreadbeasts on us as well?'

Lilith's snake eyes glittered with amusement. 'Oh, I knew you'd be fine, Tomasina, dear. You think I hadn't researched you? You think I don't know all about your circus talents?' She turned to glare at Jinx. 'This stupid boy turned out to be less easily killable than I'd hoped, however.'

'You can't kill Jinx – Lucifer would rip you to shreds,' I said hurriedly. 'And anyway, aren't you trying to get back together with Lucifer? Killing his youngest son isn't going to help with that. Or are you plotting to take over from him? Not that we really care either way.'

Lilith laughed. 'Take over from Lucifer? Hah. How very wrong you are. And my love life is my own business,' she added. 'Although if I *were* trying to get back together with my ex-husband, it might be a lot easier without a reminder of his annoying second wife around.'

Jinx turned pale pink.

'Yet you seem to be immune to spikemoths and monstrous kittens and staircase collapses, Jinx. Most irritating.' She turned to me and smiled. 'Now, Tommy dear, you're going to go and pick up a box for me,' she said.

'I am not.'

'Oh, I think you are.' She snapped her fingers and there was a slow grinding sound. A circular piece of stone floor slid aside. 'Because if you don't, Lucifer will find his son's cold, lifeless body in the palace grounds tomorrow morning. He'll be upset, of course, but he'll get over it. He'll blame the gargoyles, and that'll be that. It's all nice and neat.'

I went cold.

Lilith nodded and in one quick movement the snakes slid across the floor and disappeared down the hole with Jinx.

I heard him yell for help then the floor slid back and there was silence.

My stomach dropped out from under me. 'Don't you dare hurt him. Don't you dare.'

'Oh you really shouldn't dare me, my dear. I rather like a good dare. Still, as I said, you do your part and I'll let the brat live.' She shrugged. 'I mean, I am rather annoyed at what he did to Dantalion, but I have hundreds more children. They all blur into each other a bit.'

*Oh Loiter,* I thought, *where are you?* Then I remembered the dreadbeasts chasing us, and the creepy graffiti. It had all been near his house. *Oh no.* No, that was ridiculous, Loiter would never betray us. I had to trust that he'd be back.

Lilith, on the other hand, I didn't trust as far as I could throw her, which I really, really wanted to do at that moment, preferably into a Sarlacc Pit. But there was nothing I could do. I'd have to at least pretend to agree, then hope a plan would come to me on the way.

'OK,' I said. 'I'll do it. But first I need to know – why do you need it?'

Lilith shook her head, a small smile on her lips. 'I thought we agreed – villain speeches are so clichéd.'

The snakes slid away from me, taking my weapon belt with them, and I scrambled to my feet. Behind me the double doors creaked open.

Lilith gestured towards them. 'Have a nice time. I'll see you when you have my box. Don't go and get yourself killed now. That would be most inconvenient.'

251

What else could I do? I stepped through the doors.

They slammed shut behind me and I clenched my fists. I felt horribly, terribly alone. This was so not the way things were supposed to go.

I patted my clothes down hurriedly checking for any remaining snakes. Why was it always snakes? Then I looked up. Before me stretched a vast cavern, so vast I couldn't see the other side, lit by thousands of twinkling lights in the roof.

No. Not lights. *Eyes.* Eyes reflecting back at me.

Brilliant. That's what I got for wishing I wasn't alone.

'I don't have time for any more monsters right now!' I yelled up at them. Silently. In my head. Not wanting to frighten them or anything.

Dark, eerie water lapped at my toes. The Black Lake. It was totally just the chill in the air making me shiver. I tried to remember what Jinx had told me. Before…before he was taken. I couldn't think about that now. I had to finish this. It was the only way.

*'Memories are dangerous?'*

*'The wrong ones, yes. They can suck you in and never let you out again.'*

I looked out over the inky waters. And then, in the faint glimmer of light, a face swam into view just beneath the surface and I smacked my hand over my mouth to stifle a scream.

*Memories.* They were only memories.

Although the memories of humans who ended up in Hell wouldn't be light and fluffy, I was pretty sure. Some of my own memories certainly weren't.

But Jinx needed me, and I needed to get to the box and destroy it. If Lilith had gone to this much trouble to get it back, I dreaded to think what powers it held.

A small wooden canoe bobbed at the edge of the rocks, a lantern on a pole stuck to the front, oars lying on the bottom. I took a deep breath and stepped into it.

The whispering of the skulls had gone and it was deathly silent. I rowed into the lake, trying not to look down at the black water or up at the eyes in the roof. Talk about being stuck between a rock and a hard place. I muttered to myself as I pushed the water back and forth. If it wasn't snakes, it was bats, if it wasn't bats it was dead people. For an instant I remembered the few moments I'd spent in Heaven. Me and my brilliant ideas. *Choose Hell, Tommy, that's a brilliant idea. That devil's such a nice guy.* Shame about his scheming evil ex-wife.

But if I'd been safely in Heaven, Lilith would have killed my mum and sent her to Hell, I just knew it. It would've been her making this journey now, and she wouldn't have had the help I had. Or the help I might have, if Loiter or Jinx or anyone came to my rescue. Well, at least there was the very small hypothetical chance someone might come to my rescue.

The air grew cold and damp, and clung to me like unhappy memories. *Oh no.* I shook my arms and shoulders and looked around. A greenish, rotting face swam into view, and then another, and another. I ignored them and plunged on and on over the lake. And then the silence was interrupted by a low humming noise. I risked a glance up at the ceiling but whatever the creatures were they weren't moving.

The humming got louder and louder, and I realised it wasn't in the cavern at all. It was in my head. My vision swam and my head pounded. *No.* I pushed harder at the oars, skimming faster and faster over all the dead faces peering up at me. Then a face I recognised rippled into view. *My* face.

The cavern vanished.

I was back in my trailer on Earth, pressing my nose against the window. I looked down at my hands. They were tiny. Outside, birds chirped and sunshine beamed and blue skies smiled down at me, and I was overcome with an overwhelming longing for Earth. Then I saw a small red car and realised what I was longing for. It was my mother driving away.

No. *You're not here, you're not here,* I told myself. *You have to get back to the Black Lake.* This was the day my mother had abandoned me and I didn't want to remember it. I clenched my eyes tight shut and took a deep breath. But when I opened them I was still there in the trailer – only I was growing colder and colder. I had to wake up. I ran out of the trailer and down the steps. The grass outside came up to my knees. The sun beat down but I was shaking with cold. The red car was almost out of sight now. *No, Mum, don't go, please don't go.* I ran towards the road, my steps stumbling, my feet numb.

Suddenly I yelped in pain. And again. It was like an electric shock. I shook my head as the fields before me blurred. *Mum.* The fields vanished and darkness reared up before me. I was back in Hell. Sparky sat on my knee, throwing out sparks.

'*Sparky.* Thank you, thank you. You saved my skin.' One oar was floating across the water. I reached out and grabbed it and started to row again, but the memory of the blue skies kept flashing up into my mind.

I pushed it back down again, gritted my teeth, and rowed on.

Up ahead I saw a glimmering green light, and a rocky shoreline came into view. As I drew nearer I could see a stone wall rising up behind the rocks, and in front of the wall was a statue in an alcove. The edge of the boat clashed against the rocks and I jumped out and scrambled back away from the lake. The humming in my head melted slowly away and I breathed a huge sigh of relief. OK, one impossible thing

down. Now all I had to do was get Pandora's Box, give it to Lilith, save Jinx, then get the box back again and destroy it. Oh and get out of this hellhole. How hard could it be?

There was a clattering noise behind me. I spun round and shrieked. Dozens of ghoulish, rotting corpses were dragging themselves out of the lake towards me.

Including the one with my face.

Except her nose was sunken and her eyes were weeping blood. I screamed louder and ran along the stone wall. There was no door in it. A hand grabbed my ankle and I stomped on it with a crunch. *No.* I had to get out, I had to save Jinx, I had to... I darted back and looked more closely at the statue in the alcove. It was a woman with long hair. Her right hand was held up, palm out, like she was stopping traffic. In her right hand she held a box. *Pandora.*

There had to be some kind of mechanism... I ran my hands over the box but it was solid marble. Behind me, I could hear the lake ghouls dragging themselves across the rocks towards me, sucking and slithering and crunching. I fiddled around at the base of the statue, my heart hammering in my chest, but nothing happened.

Some kind of mechanism that only I could open, because I was descended from Pandora. That's why Lilith had gone to all this trouble.

But what if Lilith was wrong?

'Work, dammit, why won't you work?' I threw a kick at the nearest corpse and his jaw exploded in a shower of bone fragments.

I looked up at the figure's outstretched hand. *Wait.* I raised my palm and pressed it against hers. For a second nothing happened...then stone grew warm and for an instant I thought the statue's eyes glowed yellow – and it swung forward and to the side, revealing a gap in the wall.

I hung my head in relief.

'Loiter, if you're out there, now would be a really good time to come and rescue us,' I whispered. Then I leapt away from the slithering monsters and through the hole in the wall.

Percival was having the best night of his life. And since he was 2039, that was saying something. The film had been fantastic. Not because he cared about dragons or small human boys, but because Alethea had giggled and grinned her way through the entire thing and he'd sat watching her out of the corner of his eye, hardly believing his luck.

Then they'd wandered through the glowing streets of Pandemonium, and when he'd finally plucked up courage to take her hand in his, she hadn't let go for the rest of the evening. Now they were sitting on the balcony of a bar drinking Bloody Marys made with actual blood and talking like they'd known each other all their lives.

'I've had such a lovely evening,' said Alethea. 'And it was so thoughtful of you to pick a film you thought I'd enjoy.'

Percival squinted at her. 'I didn't choose the film. You did. Although I'm happy you enjoyed it.'

Alethea looked at him oddly. 'They told me you asked to meet me at the cinema. I...I don't understand.'

'They?'

'The kids. Lucifer's son Jinx and that Bonehead friend of his, Tommy. They're ever so sweet.'

Percival held his breath. 'Oh,' he said finally, 'of course. How silly of me.' He didn't know what was going on. but whatever it was, he didn't want to ruin the evening. So the kids had decided to match-make a bit. Or was there more to it? It was the Bonehead girl. His blood ran cold. Did she know about him?

Alethea smiled at him, her dark eyes glinting in the lights from the bar, and all at once he knew. She was the one for him. They were meant for each other, and if they were meant for each other, he could tell her anything.

'Actually,' he said, 'there's something I need to tell you.' He explained about the match-making kids, but when he said how pleased he was that they'd done it, because he'd been watching her for days and hadn't had the courage to talk to her before, Alethea grinned from ear to ear. And that made him even bolder. So he told her his secret. He never had been any good at keeping secrets.

'You tempted a human child?' she said when he was finished.

'Please don't hate me. I know it's against the rules but

it was an order. Lilith's a pretty fierce boss, you know.'

'No, no, of course. It's not your fault. So now you've found out, what are you going to do about it?'

Do about it? Percival had thought he'd known what he was going to do about it – keep well out of trouble until they left Hell and hope that no one ever found out. But now Alethea was looking up at him with her big eyes, he felt completely differently. He felt... brave. He would tell Lucifer all about it and beg for forgiveness and—

A rush of blue hellfire appeared on the balcony a few feet away and a bartender dropped the tray of cocktails he was carrying with a crash. Lilith ignored him and strode over to Percival's table. Percival gulped. How could she know? He'd literally only thought about it this minu—

'Are you on a date?' sneered Lilith.

'Um, well, yes, Your Highness, I...'

She waved her hand and cut him off. 'Whatever. You'll have to cut it short – something's come up.'

Alethea looked at Lilith, alarmed.

'Now.'

'Yes, of course, Your Fiendishness.'

'Meet me in the Bone Quarry.' She vanished in

261

*another whoosh of blue flames.*

*Percival turned to Alethea and took her hand. 'I'm so sorry, duty calls. Thank you for a wonderful evening. See you tomorrow?'*

*She smiled. 'That would be lovely. But why would you need to go to the Bone Quarry?'*

*He shrugged. 'Something to do with the contest, I suppose.'*

*Alethea squeezed his bony hand and his heart soared. 'Be careful.'*

*One rickshaw ride, several uncomfortable moments in the Devouring Sands and a short jog through the Bone Quarry later, Percival was standing in the crypt beneath the main hall, surrounded by snakes.*

*And gaping at Lucifer's youngest son – the boy who had helped set up the best night of his life – locked in a cage.*

*'I need you to watch over him and make sure he doesn't escape,' said Lilith.*

He's in a cage in a crypt beneath the Bone Quarry surrounded by snakes, *thought Percival,* I'm pretty sure that's impossible, *but he just nodded.*

*'Of course, Your Highness.'*

*'I'll be back soon.' She vanished.*

Percival looked suspiciously at the boy, who sat in the cage glaring at him, his face pinched and miserable.

'Did you have a nice evening?' Jinx said eventually.

'Why did you do that?' asked Percival.

Jinx sighed. 'We needed to get into your room to look at the itinerary for the contest. I'm sorry. But Lilith is up to something really bad and we need to stop her.'

'Is it something to do with your Bonehead friend?'

'How did you know? Do you know all about Pandora?'

'Who's Pandora?'

Jinx looked at him for a moment. 'You really don't know, do you? Lilith is using Tommy to get Pandora's Box. That's why Tommy's in Hell, even though she's just a kid. But I don't know why Lilith wants the box.'

Neither of them said anything for a few minutes.

'I did, thank you,' said Percival suddenly.

'You did what?'

'Have a nice evening. Even if you were just trying to get me out of the way...'

'We were. Trying to get you out of the way. But we also knew Alethea had a crush on you. It made her really happy, and we like Alethea. So I'm glad for her.'

'But you don't like me?' said Percival.

'That depends. How do you feel about helping

me escape?'

Percival thought about the secret hanging so heavy on his heart, and how much he wanted it gone. He thought about how if he helped Lucifer's son to safety, Lucifer just might be so grateful he'd forget about all the trouble with the Bonehead girl. Maybe Percival would even get to stay in Hell with Alethea.

He took a deep breath and walked over to the cage. 'I feel quite favourably inclined towards it,' he said.

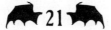

# 21

# The Daggers of the Earth

TOMMY

'WHAT ON EARTH?'

I don't know what I'd expected to find on the other side of the wall. A vast cavern full of glittering treasures, maybe, like in *Aladdin*, or a box sitting on a pedestal guarded by some ferocious hellbeast.

Instead was a high-ceilinged room, flagstones beneath my feet, with no skulls or skeletons or hellbeasts to be seen. At the far end, rising up so high I couldn't see the top, was a wall full of little niches, like a catacomb. But instead of bones in the holes, each gap held a box. I trod warily across the floor, expecting a new barrage of ghouls or monsters to appear any moment, or spikes to thrust up out of the ground, but it was quiet.

I reached the other side and looked up at the boxes. Each one was different. I sighed. I guessed I was going to have to find the right one. Why did everyone around here have to be so keen on riddles?

There was a sudden flash of orange light and I jumped back. 'Loiter! Thank heavens. Where did you go, did you—'

'Tommy! I can't talk, Lilith persuaded a coven of humans to summon me. I'm so sorry, I keep getting dragged back to Earth. I'll try to fetch—'

He vanished again. I swore loudly. Lucifer had his hands full fighting off the gargoyle infestation and Loiter was being kept busy on Earth. Lilith really had thought of everything. Well, it was just going to have to be down to me. I clenched my fists. She wouldn't get away with this. I'd think of something.

I looked at all the boxes along the bottom ledge. Two looked like they were made of solid gold. Well, that was no good. Gold was soft, I knew, because when I'd been in the circus the Strong Lady had kept breaking her favourite bracelet. What had Jinx said? Pandora had tried lots of different materials before finding one that was strong enough to forge an unbreakable box. I looked at the boxes at shoulder height. Here they were iron or some kind of silver metal. But iron probably would've been one of the first materials Pandora had tried, so it wouldn't be that. Anyway, iron rusted. I looked up. *Badgers.* I was going to have to climb.

I'd mostly got over my fear of heights since coming to

Hell, thanks to a tiny incident with Jinx and a mountainside, and having a huge amount of fun being flown around by dragons. But sitting safely in a carriage was different from climbing what looked like a very crumbly rock wall. But there was no other way up. I gritted my teeth and started to climb.

Luckily some of the holes in the wall were big enough for me to climb into and catch my breath. I tried not to look down. I found an oak box, a mahogany chest, and an old leather suitcase that seemed like someone else had thought of the demonic suitcase joke. Almost twenty feet off the ground, I found the biggest niche yet. The box was the size of a coffin, and was made with numerous different-coloured metals woven into one another. I grinned. This had to be it. Pandora had found a way to tie lots of different metals together to make them stronger. I crawled over to it, tripped on a rock and fell on top of it.

And squished it flat. I could've cried. So, not this one then. I crawled back out and started climbing again. I reached gingerly up for the next level and the rock beneath my toe crumbled. I shrieked and grabbed onto the hole above but instead I grabbed the box inside. It was light and rather than yanking myself up I pulled it out and it fell past my head and landed on the stone floor far below. With my second try I grabbed the ledge and climbed into the now empty niche.

I leant back against the wall and sucked in a deep breath. Then I took Sparky out of my pocket and shook my head. 'This is going to take all day,' I grumbled.

Sparky threw out a few sparks.

'It's *not* going to take all day? Well, that's a relief.' I scooched along out of the niche on my belly and looked down...and noticed something odd.

The box that I had accidentally thrown over my head had not shattered to bits. In fact, it was still in one very solid piece. I stared.

'Sparky, is that Pandora's Box? I mean, *that is Pandora's Box.*'

Sparky stayed non-electricky. That was it! I'd found it.

I clambered carefully back down to ground level and ran over to the box. *Bamboo.* It was made of bamboo. Then I remembered how we'd often put up our tents at the circus with bamboo, because it was so strong and so flexible. Of course. What else had Jinx said? *The daggers of the earth.* Bamboo was very sharp when you cut it at an angle. So that would make sense. I picked it up. The box was twice the size of a suitcase, but it was light. Now I just had to get rid of it before Lilith—

'Not bad. Not bad at all.'

I spun round. Lilith stepped through the opening to the Black Lake, smiling like the cat who'd got the cream, then drowned all her enemies in it.

I backed away, gripping the box. 'Set Jinx free. Then you can have it.'

'My dear, stupid child. Do you honestly think I couldn't take it from you in an instant?'

I looked around wildly. I needed a way to destroy it. But how was I supposed to destroy an unbreakable box? I really wished I hadn't put off planning that bit. 'Set him free. You promised.'

She laughed. 'Do I look like the sort of person who keeps her promises?'

'Well, now that you mention it, not really.'

'I should hope not.'

'You could always turn over a new leaf.'

'I don't think so.' She flicked a glance to the side and snakes poured from cracks in the ceiling and floors, hissing and spitting.

I backed away till I was right up against the wall. 'Why?' I said, stalling for time, stalling for Loiter, stalling for any kind of brainwave that would get me out of this mess. 'Why do you want the box so badly? What's in it?'

She wagged a finger at me. 'I told you before. I'm not a fan of speeches.'

There was a flash of blue light and the box was ripped from my grasp.

# She Who Must Not Be Named

TOMMY

'LOITER!' I YELLED, as though it would do any good. 'Loiter, help!'

Lilith rolled her eyes. 'Do you think I wouldn't take precautions? I know you managed to foil Dantalion's little rebellion. I didn't underestimate you, child. Scream all you want. Your furry friend isn't coming to your rescue.'

'But I am!' yelled a voice, and a small figure sprang out from behind a pillar and drove a dagger into Lilith's back.

'Jinx!'

Lilith dropped the box and spun round, trying to reach the dagger sticking out of her shoulder blades. She roared in fury. Jinx picked up the box and we ran for the exit. The ground rumbled. I threw a glance over my shoulder and yelped.

Where Lilith had stood was now a towering green

serpent with red eyes. And it didn't look happy. Its tail came crashing across the floor and smashed straight into Jinx, sending him and the box flying. He landed with a moan. *Weapons,* dammit. If only I still had my weapons. I leaped over the tail and slid behind a pillar.

Lilith's voice came from the snake, more slithery than ever. 'Oh I am going to enjoy this,' it said as it swept across the floor to Jinx.

I looked up at the torches in the walls but they were too high for me to reach. I ran at the nearest pillar, bounced off it and caught my hand in the iron bracket holding the torch. I grabbed it, sprang back down and pelted across the room to Jinx, but Lilith flicked her tail at me and extinguished the flame. Her scaly green head rose from the ground and her jaws opened, revealing a black forked tongue and razor-sharp fangs as long as fence posts.

Jinx grabbed the box and held it in front of him just as she swooped, and her fangs bounced off it. He leapt to his feet and backed away, holding the box up like a shield.

Then the weirdest thing happened. The fiend called Percival ran into the room and jumped onto the serpent's back.

'How dare you?' hissed Lilith, trying to throw him off.

'I never did like you,' stammered Percival, 'and...and

you're a terrible boss!' He stabbed at her with some kind of spear.

Lilith slid backwards and slammed into a pillar with a crunch. Percival slid to the floor, blue blood pouring from his head, his neck twisted at an odd angle. His eyes stared unseeing at the ceiling. Oh *no*.

I ran at the next pillar along, bounced to get another torch and stuck my hand right in the flame. I screeched but grabbed it anyway and fell back to the floor. My ankle folded under me and I heard a crack. When I tried to stand on it tears sprung up in my eyes.

I hopped up and leant against a pillar, brandishing the torch in front of me. The snake's tail swished hard across the floor and threw the box out of Jinx's hands. Then Lilith raised her scaly head once more.

'I do like to work up an appetite before dinner,' she hissed.

I hopped towards Jinx as quickly as I could and stuck the flame into her tail but she smacked into me and I landed in a crumpled heap, howling with pain.

'Yes, yes,' said Lilith. 'You gave it your best shot. Now please shut up and die.' She sped down towards Jinx, scales gleaming in the torchlight. Jinx rolled away just in time and her fangs smacked into the ground. He was only a few feet from the door to the Black Lake now.

'Get out of here!' I yelled. 'Just run, Jinx!'

He hesitated, looking at me, slumped on the floor, and then at the door – and in that instant Lilith swooped and Jinx disappeared behind her head. I screamed.

All at once a blinding flash of purple light filled the air, and Lilith flew across the room.

'Don't you touch my son!' said a furious voice.

Standing in the centre of the room was a woman I had never seen before. Where Lilith had been beautiful in a dark, terrifying way, like moonlight on a guillotine, this woman was as radiant as springtime. Her long brown hair was wound with daisies and her deep pink dress was made entirely of freesias. Her eyes glinted blue in her dark brown face.

'Mum!' gasped Jinx.

So this was Persephone. She had finally come home.

Lilith picked herself up and slithered to her full height. 'You,' she hissed.

Persephone's eyes narrowed. 'It's so undignified to chase after a man who doesn't want you,' she said.

'He's mine! He's always been mine! You were just a stupid dalliance.'

Persephone smiled. 'So he's welcomed you back with

open arms, has he?'

The serpent's eyes flickered. 'He will. You've warped him, he's not the demon he once was. Once I open Pandora's Box and destroy humanity, he will remember his old self. He will remember how much he hates the humans. And he will return to me.'

So *that* was what she wanted. Trust a demon to make a Valentine present of destroying humanity. What was wrong with a nice box of chocolates?

Lilith charged and Persephone magicked bamboo shoots from her hands and fired them at her. Lilith howled, looking like a porcupine.

'Fighting me with flowers,' she snarled, 'how sweet.'

'Turning into a giant snake,' countered Persephone, 'how clichéd. And just how are you going to destroy humanity with an empty box?'

'It's not empty, you pathetic flower girl. Don't you know your legends? All the evils *but one* were released. Released by me. I kept the final one as a weapon.'

'Didn't do a very good job of hanging onto your final weapon, did you? Bit careless to lose it,' said Jinx.

Lilith spat venom at him, orange and stringy, and he threw himself out of the way as it burned into the flagstones.

'I didn't lose it, you idiot. I put it here.'

'Behind a door only Pandora or one of her bloodline could open?' said Persephone. 'That was clever.'

'Pandora tricked her way into Hell. She locked the box away from me. Away from all demonkind!'

She lashed her tail out at Persephone but the goddess disappeared and reappeared behind her, with a fistful of vines that she wound round and round Lilith's long body, tighter and tighter. The snake started to gasp for breath.

Lilith started to gasp for breath. 'Pandora got her comeuppance, though. Now she's... nothing but stone,' she wheezed.

I froze. The statue at the entrance hadn't been a statue at all. It had been Pandora herself. Lilith had turned her to stone, but somehow Pandora had succeeded in blocking the entrance as she died.

Persephone laughed, and it was like glass chimes in the wind. 'Oh, I bet your face was a picture, Lilith, dear. Chase your little human all the way to the depths of Hell – and she defeats you even in death.'

'Wasn't part of the plan, it has to be said,' grumbled the towering serpent. 'She wasn't supposed to have any powers.'

'Dying wishes have their own power,' said Persephone, raising her hand and pulling the vines even tighter around Lilith's thrashing body. 'Don't you know that by now? I've

seen it many times with humans. She died wanting to protect the box so badly that her wish came true.'

'Not true any more,' hissed Lilith. 'I will destroy you all, then with the box I will destroy humanity and...my love will return to me,' she panted.

Behind her, Jinx saw his moment. He picked up Pandora's Box and ran over to me. 'We have to destroy this,' he whispered.

The pain in my ankle was eating away at me so I could hardly think. 'How do we break an unbreakable box? It won't even burn. Plus we still don't know what's in it. We don't want to accidentally let out the only remaining evil and destroy humanity. That would be a bit of a bummer.'

'What is it?' spat Persephone at Lilith. 'What's in the box?'

Lilith roared and the vines binding her serpentine body snapped. 'Despair, of course. I thought death and war and pestilence would crush the human spirit forever. But no, those little insects can survive anything, anything, so long as they have hope. Who knew?' She reared up and the rest of the vines fell from her body.

'But without hope, oh, they cannot exist. Despair is the antihope. It will suck every last morsel of joy and self-belief from them. They cannot survive without it. They will drown in their own misery.'

I stared at Jinx. 'They will drown... Jinx, that's it!'

He shoved his shoulder under my arm and lifted me up. 'What's it?'

I cupped my hand over his ear. 'The Black Lake,' I whispered. 'It's bottomless. We have to throw the box in the lake!'

Jinx picked up the box with his free hand and we hobbled across to the hole in the wall. Behind us there was a crunch and we spun round in time to see Lilith land a blow across Persephone's waist, sending her flying.

Jinx winced but within an instant his mother was back on her feet, fire in her eyes.

'You shouldn't have done that,' she said, in a low, menacing voice. She stepped forward and raised her arms. Petals dropped from her hair and her dress began to smoke.

Goosebumps rose on my skin.

Persephone was changing.

The smoke whirled round and round her and lifted her up into the air like a tornado. Now her hair shimmered dark blue, and her fingers lengthened into pointed metal claws like swords. Her eyes flashed fire, and electricity crackled out from the smoke like lightning. She was no longer the sweet spring goddess. The Queen of the Dead had come home.

'Get. Out. Of. My. House!' she roared, sending a blast of blue lightning at Lilith.

I tugged Jinx's arm. 'Come on!'

Jinx stepped through the hole with the box and I fell through after him.

'Told you my mum was badass,' he said.

Badass didn't even begin to describe it. 'Why was Percival with you?' I asked.

'It's OK,' said Jinx, 'he's on our side.'

A *fiend* was on our side? This day was getting weirder and weirder.

'Or he was,' I said, thinking of his blank eyes.

Through the gap in the wall I saw Lilith come barrelling towards us.

'Jinx, hurry!'

He raised the box over his head and threw it as far as he could into the lake.

Where it floated merrily on top.

My blood ran cold. 'Oh no, *no*...it's bamboo, of course it floats, what are we—'

Lilith oozed through the hole, knocking Jinx out of the way. He flew through the air and smacked hard into the stone platform. I gasped and shrank back, staring between his crumpled form and the floating box in the middle of the lake. Now what?

Persephone whirled to a stop beside me, a creature of smoke and blades and flashing electricity. Not a creature – a goddess. She looked out across the Black Lake and held out her hands palms up. 'In memoriam,' she whispered.

A ragged, rotten arm reached up out of the water – then another, and another. Slowly the ghouls of the Black Lake dragged the box down into the depths.

'No!' shrieked Lilith, and dived headlong into the dark water.

Persephone and I rushed over to Jinx. His head lolled and I fought back tears. Then he opened his eyes and smiled wanly at us.

'Did we win?'

'I don't know.'

The three of us stared after Lilith. Bubbles rose up on the inky surface, then more, and more. There was a fight going on underwater.

'I bet Lilith has some really nasty memories,' I said hopefully.

The bubbling on the lake began to die down, until finally it ebbed away completely. The Black Lake fell silent.

'Is that it? Is she really gone?' I asked Persephone.

'Let's make sure, shall we?' she said. She walked to the edge of the rocks, took a deep breath, and blew. And as she blew, her breath turned the lake to ice, jagged and black and sparkling.

'That should do it,' she said. She shook her arms and the blades became fingers once more. Then she turned and scooped Jinx up in her arms. 'What has your father been letting you get up to?' she said, her face stern.

Jinx grinned. 'Mum, you have the best timing.'

She looked over at me, her blue hair shining, light crackling all around her. 'And you must be Tommy. Jinx has told me all about you.'

There was a blinding flash of red light and I jumped. But it was only Lucifer, wings flaming, hands held up in fists like he was ready to fight. 'What happened? Where is she? Just wait until I—'

Persephone burst out laughing and put her hand on his arm. 'Don't worry, darling, us girls have got this.'

# Epilogue

## JINX

DAD RAISED HIS glass and smiled. 'A very happy Saturnalia to one and all.'

The royal apartments glittered with candles, which Sparky was winding through and gleefully lighting. A mountain of presents sat beneath the statue of Saturn that was wheeled out every year, which Mum had decorated with a party hat, beads, and garlands of black roses. I stood warming my tail in front of the huge stone fireplace that was the centrepiece of the drawing room, belly stuffed full of every delicacy known to demonkind. Tommy lay on a sofa, the cast around her ankle covered in red and gold glitter to match her party dress, and Mum and Dad sat on another, mooning at each other. Loiter was sprawled across an armchair, glass of wine in his paw.

The gargoyles had come to their senses the minute Lilith had disappeared beneath the Black Lake, but before then they'd totally trashed our rooms, so Dad had brought Tommy and me to stay in his part of the palace. There were no spikemoths here, although there was no Slaystation either, sadly. I couldn't fault Mum's festive spirit, though. Everywhere hung red and gold decorations of little devils and goblins and boxes with ribbons. Even Bruce dangled upside down from Saturn's outstretched arm like a belated Halloween ornament.

'Happy Saturnalia to you too, my darling,' said Mum, her blue hair shimmering like an Earthly predawn sky, her smile wide as the moon. She kissed Dad on the cheek. 'And to how much your taste in wives has improved over the years.'

'I'll drink to that,' I said, laughing.

'To the end of Pandora's Box,' said Loiter, taking a swig of mulled wine.

'I'll drink to that,' said Tommy, holding up her glass of grimberry juice.

There was a knock on the door and a crowd of guests tumbled into the room, led by a nervous-looking Percival, his head bandaged, and a shyly smiling Alethea. Dad stood up.

'Welcome, welcome!'

Mum pressed glasses of mulled wine into their hands.

'To best friends,' I said, holding my glass of banana milk out towards Tommy.

'And to best fiends,' said Dad, toasting Percival. 'Have you given some more thought to my offer?'

Percival shuffled his feet. 'It's very kind of you, Your Majesty.

Just a few weeks ago, being head of all the fiends would have been more than I could ever have imagined.' He glanced at Alethea. 'But now...well, if it's OK with you, Your Majesty, I'd like to stay in Hell. Alethea would hate to leave her dragons.'

Dad nodded. 'And I would have a hard time finding a new dragon handler as talented.'

Alethea blushed beneath her green skin.

'So!' said Mum. 'Who's up for charades?'

'Presents first!' I said.

She rolled her eyes. 'Of course, presents first.'

285

'That reminds me,' said Dad, looking at me and Tommy. 'I have a special present for you two. Come with me.' He nodded at Mum. 'We'll be right back.'

We followed him out of the apartments and through the palace. Everywhere hung decorations and winding green lights and little bells that chimed as we passed. We came to the bottom of the stairs leading up to our rooms.

'The serfs finished renovating today,' he said. 'Your rooms are ready.' He led us into my room. Last time I'd seen it, it had been a mess of rubble and broken glass. Now everything was as good as new. There was even a hammock hanging from the rafters and...

'Is that a new Slaystation?' I said, running over.

'It is. Couple of games to go with it, too.'

'Thanks, Dad.'

He turned to Tommy. 'Your room is ready too. Not that I'm in any hurry to have you two out of the apartments, of course, but...'

I smirked. 'But you want to spend the next six months making googly eyes at Mum.'

'Shhh. Don't tell anyone.'

We followed him along the covered bridge and into Tommy's room. I gasped. Where the broken glass had been was a stained glass window. A stained glass window showing a fierce-looking Tommy, blonde plaits flying out, a throwing star clutched in one hand, a tiny shocktopus in the other throwing off sparks. Beneath, in old-fashioned calligraphy, were the words 'Tomasina D'Evil'.

'This...this is for me?' she said, looking bewildered.

Dad bent down to Tommy's height and put his hands on her shoulders. 'I've told you before you are one of the family, but I'm not sure you believed me,' he said gently. 'You've saved my son's life more times than I can count. On top of that, I like you. There are no circumstances under which I'd send you away, do you understand? None. This is your home now.'

Tommy broke into a wobbly smile. She nodded.

'So I thought we should officially adopt you. Persephone's idea, actually. What do you say? I think Tomasina D'Evil has a nice ring to it.'

Tommy bit her lip hard and tears welled up in her eyes. 'Thank you,' she mumbled.

I grinned. 'Now you're my little sister I really get to torture you,' I said.

She shook her head. 'Oh no. No more torture, or death-defying stunts, or crazy adventures. I've had my fill of those.'

'Really?' said Dad. 'That is a shame. The annual New Year's dragon races are coming up, and I rather thought you might like to join up with Alethea.'